Life

and

Lemonade

Renaissance

Cover art and design by Nathan Frechette. Layout by Nathan Fréchette. Edited by Meghan Côté, Myryam Ladouceur, Victoria Martin, Ev Cimesa, Cait Gordon, Talia Johnson and Nathan Fréchette.

Legal deposit, Library and Archives Canada, May 2018.

Paperback ISBN: 978-1-987963-36-6
Ebook ISBN 978-1-987963-37-3

Renaissance Press
Pressesrenaissancepress.ca

Life

and

Lemonade

~ A Novel ~

Jamieson Wolf

This book is for Michael.
Thank you for loving me and letting me
love you.

Chapter One

"I want a divorce."

Romilda stood back to let Cordellia enter. Cordellia still had the power to take her breath away. Even after all these years, she reminded Romilda of a younger Shirley MacLaine. "Well hello to you, too, dear. No 'hi there, how has it been?' or 'Wow, you look fantastic!'"

"Sorry, it's been on my mind all morning and I thought I would burst if I didn't get it out." Cordellia walked past her and made her way to the kitchen. "I need a drink."

"You need a drink? You haven't just been handed your dick on a platter."

Cordellia gave Romilda a shrewd look. "That's funny, seeing as you no longer have one."

"A mere technicality," Romilda said. Walking to the kitchen, she took down two champagne flutes.

"What are you doing? Aren't we going to have wine?"

"Sweetheart, I always have wine. When my wife of nearly forty years asks me for a divorce, it deserves champagne."

"I haven't been your wife for a long time, Romilda."

"You know what I mean. You obviously want the divorce for a reason. Who's the lucky man?"

Romilda tried to keep her back straight, stand tall, and seem happy. The truth she felt taken aback, in shock. Cordellia had been a constant for her in a world that had changed completely. Though Romilda had decided to change it herself, to live as her true self and not a lie, was beside the point.

"It's Joe," Cordellia quietly stated. "It's always been Joe."

The knife went a little deeper. "I know," Romilda nodded

sadly. "What I don't understand is why you ran away from him. You were having an affair, everything was going so well. He could have been father to Blaine. Why did you leave him?"

"I was still messed up when you left, when you chose to become what you did. I needed to be alone."

"Honey, I wanted you to have a life when I left—not live like a nun."

"I had Blaine. That was enough."

"What changed? Why now?"

Cordellia took her time answering. Finally, she looked Romilda in the eyes and said, "I was tired of being alone when my heart always belonged to Joe."

Romilda took a deep shuddering breath. "So, when's the big date?"

"Date?"

"Yes, I assume he asked you to marry him?"

"No, he hasn't yet."

"What do you mean?"

"I still haven't been to see him. He doesn't know how I feel or that I know where he is."

Romilda looked at her with shock. "Then why the hell are you coming here to ask for a divorce?"

"I want my life back. I want my heart back. Only then can I give it to someone else."

Nodding, Romilda put the champagne flutes away and took down two ordinary wine glasses. "Right, in that case, we'll wait on the champagne."

"Why?"

"We'll have the champagne when you say 'yes' to him, when he proposes. For now, we're going to celebrate you reclaiming your independence with wine and getting shit-faced. That sound good to you?"

Cordellia laughed and the sound still reminded Romilda of bells ringing. "Perfect."

Chapter Two

"So, what do you bitches want to drink?" Nancy glanced over at Chuck.

Chuck was still a man's man, but being in love with Sebastian had softened him. His eyes no longer had that hungry expression, always looking for the next fuck. Now he just seemed happy. "I'll have a screwdriver."

"That's funny," interjected Sebastian. "I thought I already gave you one of those."

"Ha ha, funny man, what do you want?"

"A glass of red."

"That's an awfully tame choice," Nancy said with a grin.

"Well, there has to be some class in this joint, right?"

"Babe, you're meeting my friends for the first time. Play nice."

"It's all good Chuck, we like him already." Sebastian had been a surprise for all of them. He was so—there was no other word for it—normal. The men Chuck had slept with in the past had been as hungry and desperate as Chuck used to be. Sebastian had his shit together, and Nancy could tell he was nothing but good for Chuck. Sebastian balanced him.

Blaine said, "I'll have the same. You, Justin?"

Even Blaine was happier than Nancy had ever seen him. There was something in Justin that brought out the light Blaine had been hiding for so long. It was good to see it back. Nancy loved Blaine like a brother, and it was about time he had met a lover who treated him so well.

"I'll have a white wine spritzer." They all turned to look at him. "What?"

"That's a pretty gay drink, is all," Nancy said.

4

"Yeah," Mike chuckled. "It's something Nancy would order."

"That's simply not true. I'm having an alcoholic Shirley Temple!"

"Well, I did always hear she had a drinking problem, "Chuck quipped.

"Shut your mouth!" Nancy said. "That woman is a goddess!"

"You tell'em honey." Mike leaned in and kissed him. It was amazing that they had been friends for so long and, all that time, there was love underneath it all. Oh, he loved all his friends, but the fact that Mike had harboured feelings for him, real feelings, was a dream come true.

"What'll you have, babe?"

"Make that two alcoholic Shirley Temples."

"See, didn't I tell you the woman was a lush?" Chuck joked.

Nancy waved a hand at him. "Oh, stop, I can't even. Someone take him out and hose him down."

Chuck turned to Sebastian. "Well, you heard the man. Take out your hose."

"Oh please," Blaine groaned. "I just ate. I have no desire to see either of your hoses."

"So, is anyone going to tell us what we're celebrating?" Justin asked. "The suspense is killing me. You said it was big news. What is it?"

"Well, I heard back from the agent today …"

"And? What did he say?" Blaine asked.

They were all looking at him, and Nancy couldn't hold back any longer. "He sold my book to a publisher! Ladies and gentlemen, I'm going to be out in hardcover!"

"Better than just being out and hard," Chuck teased.

Chapter Three

Romilda was in shock.

Not the horrible life-ending kind of shock. More like the life-altering one that takes your breath away, and you're not sure if you'll ever catch it again. She didn't know what to do with herself after Cordellia's earth-shattering news.

Though it was still early in the evening, she poured herself another drink. Although she wasn't one for drinking often, it was either this or delve into the pack of Oreos she had sitting in the cupboard, and that wouldn't do: she was far too overweight.

Pouring herself a glass of wine, Romilda tried to think of why she was so upset. She should be happy for Cordellia, thrilled for her even. Cordellia had finally found someone who she wanted in her life. Romilda didn't know how it would go, but the fact remained that Cordellia was getting on with her life.

So, why couldn't she?

Romilda had been lonely, despite how much joy her transition had brought. It finally felt as if she was in the right body, living the right life. It was everything she had dreamed it could be and more. That's not to say that she didn't have her darker days, but those were few and far between. Her world just felt more right, somehow.

Still, she would give her whole liquor cabinet for a good fuck.

The only bright spot was Cordellia. They had been apart for so long that when they had come together again, it was like meeting for the first time. They had formed a fragile relationship at first, but it had grown into a friendship over time.

If Romilda was honest with herself, she still loved Cordellia. Romilda had always hoped that once she felt happier in her own body, the body she had always wanted, Cordellia could find a way to love her again.

She was about to pour herself another glass of wine when there was a knock on her condo door. With a sigh, Romilda set the glass and bottle back down and went to answer it. When she opened the door, he was the last person she wanted to see right now.

"Hey, good looking. Came to see if you wanted to come out for a drink with me."

Staring at Gaston, Romilda reminded herself that a lady was always polite. "Why don't you just fuck off and leave me to my wine." Then again, maybe not.

Gaston let out a healthy laugh. "You sure do know how to tell it like it is. We've lived in the same building for years. When will you come for a drink with me?"

"When pigs learn to fly without aid from technology."

"Oh, now come on. What do you have against me?"

Having never been asked the question outright, Romilda actually had to stop and think of the answer. Gaston was tall and broad shouldered, still had all of his hair and all of his teeth. He was five years older than her sixty-five years and still lived young.

Gaston was also funny and friendly and had a lot of friends in their building. He helped everyone when they needed help. He was kind and selfless, that much she could see. Shaking her head, Romilda said, "I don't know."

Letting out a chuckle, Gaston gave her a dashing smile. "You don't know? Something about me sets you on edge and has you willing to turn me down without even one date?"

Romilda let out a long breath. "That's about the size of it, I guess."

"Well, then you have some thinking to do. When you figure out why you want to turn me down without even giving me a shot, come and find me. We'll go for that drink."

He did something unexpected then. Gaston leaned in and kissed her softly on the lips. He smelled of spice and his lips were soft. When he pulled away, Romilda's lips were tingling.

"Be seeing you soon, Romy."

Leaving Romilda standing in her doorway, stuck to the spot, Gaston walked away whistling a merry tune and left her wishing for more.

Chapter Four

Poppy wondered if she could get the words she wanted to say past her lips.

They had been on her mind and on her tongue every time she looked at Dava for the past few weeks. Having a normal conversation was difficult as the words she wanted to say were so different than the words she actually spoke. She would have whole conversations with Dava and not be aware of what she'd said, all in an effort to keep the words she wanted to say inside.

It was too soon, far too soon. She couldn't feel this way, she just couldn't. So, she suffered in silence … until Dava broke the words free.

"So, are you going to tell me what's up with you?"

"Huh? What do you mean?"

"You've been distracted lately. At first, I thought you had found someone else, or were having an affair—"

"I would never!"

"Let me finish. I knew that you wouldn't do that, so I began wondering if there was something the matter with the baby, but I went with you to your last appointment, so I know there isn't anything wrong."

"Dava, honey, it's not like that."

"I know. Which leads me to believe that something is bothering you and you're just busting at the seams to keep those words in for fear of upsetting me."

"No, it's nothing like that, either!"

Poppy sat up and took Dava's hands in hers. She felt warmth and strength from that touch and gathered up some of her courage. "Dava, you know you mean more to me than anything in the whole world. In fact, you mean the world and beyond to me. I've never felt this way with anyone else."

Pulling her hands away from Poppy's, Dava crossed her arms in front of her chest. "Go on."

Poppy missed the warmth of Dava's touch instantly but, undeterred, carried on anyway. God, she was out of her depth here. "You've filled my life with a light that can't be vanquished, but it's not enough. I—"

"Oh, get on with it why don't you?"

"Get on with what?"

"Just get on with it."

Dava was angry now and Poppy had no idea why, but now that most of the words were out, she pressed on. "Will you marry me?" Poppy asked quietly.

Dava was quiet for a moment, her face filled with shock. Then she erupted in loud barks of laughter. Of all the reactions, Poppy did not expect this one. Even more quietly, she asked, "So is that a 'yes?'"

"Oh, my goodness, yes! You're really bad at that, you know?"

"Well, I've never asked someone to marry me before! What was wrong with my proposal?"

"You used three different breakup lines."

"No, I didn't!"

"Yes, you did. You mean more to me than anyone, but; I've never felt this way with anyone else, but; and finally, you fill my life with happiness, but." Dava was still chuckling. "I've heard every one of those in a breakup."

"No! Well, those people were asshats."

"That's right, and now I've got you in my life, I'm not letting you get away. Why the sudden need to get married?"

Poppy rubbed her stomach. "You'll probably think I'm just being silly."

"Why don't you try me, first?"

"Well, I don't think any child should be without two parents. I know that Cordellia did that with Blaine, but I'm nowhere near as strong as she is. Also, I can't picture my life without you and want to make a family with you. I want my child growing up knowing both of his mothers instead of just me."

Poppy's love for Dava grew when she noticed tears appearing like jewels at the corner of her eyes. However, it shook just a little when Dava spoke. "I can't marry you," she whispered.

"Listen, if it's because we've only known each other a short time …"

"It's not that." She looked like she was in pain. "I just can't marry you. Why can't we just enjoy each other for now, discover new things together. I'll always stand by you; I'm not going anywhere. But I can't marry you."

Poppy nodded and tried to keep her heart from breaking. Staring more intently at Dava and noticing how she avoided her eyes, Poppy knew she was hiding something and not telling her the whole truth.

Now she just had to figure out what that truth was.

Chapter Five

Chuck was in love. There was no other way to say it.

Even now, months later, he was marvelling at this fact. Having never been in love before Sebastian came into his life, he was a poor judge of the emotion. But everything he'd read told him that what he felt was love.

He had experienced every glorious symptom of being in love: the jitters, the nervousness, the thrills of caring that deeply for another human being. Sure, he loved Blaine, Nancy, Mike, and Justin. This was different though.

Now he was going to live with another man.

Along with loving another romantic interest, he had never lived with anyone, not even his first boyfriend, Francis. Sure, they had dated for a while, but they had never lived together. Sebastian would be the first in many respects for Chuck.

He was frightened as fuck that he would screw it up.

His possessions were all in boxes. Chuck had purged everything he thought he wouldn't need: the large collection of porn, the sling and harness. He kept the handcuffs, though; those could come in handy.

Sebastian had helped him pack everything and the big day was tomorrow. Chuck was moving into Sebastian's place. He felt odd heading into someone else's home, but Sebastian put his fears to rest. "It's not a home without you. I've only lived there for a little over a year. My home is with you, regardless of where we live."

That had calmed Chuck down a bit, but he was still nervous. As he looked at his belongings in boxes, he realized he was ending one chapter of his life and beginning a new one. This thrilled and terrified him all at once.

Sebastian saw him staring at the boxes and said, "Penny for your thoughts?"

"How about a dollar, due to inflation?"

"Fine, a dollar then. You look like a deer caught in the headlights. What's up?"

"Is it wrong that I'm afraid?"

"Afraid of what?"

"Afraid of this, us, what we're about to do. How can I love you so much but still be terrified? That's not right."

Sebastian smiled and came closer to Chuck, put his arms around him. "It's okay to be scared. It means you're human."

"Yeah?"

"Yeah. We're making a big change, you more than me."

"I highly doubt that."

"How so?"

"You decided to become a man. That's a bigger choice than the one I'm making."

Sebastian shook his head. "It wasn't a choice. I was always a man inside; he just had to be allowed out. My body was never comfortable, always wrong to me. I was just making things right. The obstetrician who delivered me screwed up and said I was a girl, but I wasn't. I was a boy — that didn't change."

"Yes, but rather than live with how you felt, you did something about it."

"And so are you. As afraid as you are, you're not running."

"No, I'm not. My life didn't begin until I met you."

"I feel the same way."

Sebastian pressed his lips to Chuck's and felt him relax into the kiss. Heat ran through him that had nothing to do with fright and everything to do with the heady mix of love and lust.

Chuck broke the kiss and smiled. "Want to take one final

tumble on the bed before we toss it tomorrow?"

"I thought you'd never ask," Sebastian huskily intoned and kissed him again.

Chapter Six

Cordellia tried to keep calm while she approached his street.

She tried but wasn't entirely successful. Her heart started beating wildly in her chest and she found it difficult to breathe. Instead of turning left down his street, she turned right to go to the little park closeby.

Cordellia knew the park well. She couldn't count the number of times she had taken Blaine and had attempted to find the courage enough to knock on his door. He had been there for Blaine's birth, but then she had run away. She had left him, had chosen to protect her broken heart rather than mend it.

Well, she was choosing love now. She loved everyone in her life, even Ernest a little bit. But she didn't love herself, not really as much as she should. Well, that would start immediately—or in five minutes—when it stopped feeling like she had a hummingbird in her chest.

Sitting on the bench, she took a few deep breaths hoping to calm her nerves. Wasn't that what every yoga person was always talking about, breathing? The whole thing seemed to be built around it. Or, there was meditation. She had never tried it. Cordellia had too much in her head to keep it quiet. She always did. She often woke from dreams in which everything in her life that had gone wrong played back before her eyes.

Letting out a breath, she tried to relax. She was supposed to be so brave. She had raised a son after her husband had left her to become a woman. If that wasn't brave, what was? And yet, here she was unable to approach the house that held the man she loved more than anything in the world. When did she become so frightful?

She closed her eyes and took another deep breath. "I can do this. I can do this. I can do this." She repeated it three times like her grandmother had taught her. She had always said, "Once for conviction, twice for intent, and three times for courage."

She nearly jumped into the air when a voice said, "Well, I'm glad you've got that decided then. What is it you're trying to do?"

Opening her eyes, Cordellia looked at a face she would have known anywhere. The man was tall, slim, and had lost none of his good physique to age. He still had a full head of hair and it was grey now, peppered with white. His chin was strong, and his smile was blinding. "Joe?" she whispered.

He nodded and sat down on the bench beside her. There were already a few children out and they were playing hide and go seek with the play structure. It was their laughter that brought her courage, that sound of purity that reminded her so much of Blaine as a child. It was a sound that she carried in her heart right next to the sound of Joe's voice.

"Cordellia …" He turned away from her and wiped at tears in his eyes. "Why are you here?"

"Would you believe it's because I'm ready now? I'm ready to let my heart love you."

"And you weren't before? Gods, it's been thirty years. Why now?"

"Because I'm ready to love myself and let myself be loved. I won't let past mistakes stand in the way of what I want, even though I'm terrified."

He sat there quietly for a while and they just listened to the children playing, their laughter like music as its notes rang into the air. Finally, Joe spoke. "There is much I'd like to say to you and I sense there's a lot that you have to say to me. The one thing that I do have to tell you is this: I have never stopped loving you, not for one moment. Did you want to go somewhere with me? I could buy us drinks, maybe some brunch?"

The hummingbird returned and instead of trying to calm it down, Cordellia let it flap its wings. "I would like that," she said rather breathlessly. "I would like that very much."

Chapter Seven

Joe took them to Dante's, a restaurant they used to visit often. It was down the street from his house and it served the best coffee in the world, made with cinnamon and spices. The food was excellent, too. Joe had brought Cordellia here when they had first started dating. It had always held a special place in his heart.

She took it all in with a smile. "It still looks the same. Same decor, same tables. Do they still have my favourite foods?" Cordellia picked up a menu and opened it gleefully.

"They do, but they've updated it quite a lot over the years."

She put down her menu and looked at him. "It must have been hard for you to come here without me."

Joe let out a bark of laughter. "Darlin', it was hard to breathe without you. One day you were with me and then you weren't. I had no idea where you had gone."

"I always knew where you were."

"How could you? I moved a few times before I found the house I'm in now."

"I asked around. The old crowd helped a bit."

"Hmmm, like Gloria and Stefan? They were always encouraging me to find you, saying that you needed me."

"I did need you, but I was too stubborn to admit it."

"What changed?"

"I changed, I think. I was there for Blaine and his crowd of friends as they all found love of one kind or another. And Blaine's friend Poppy was a driving force, really."

"How so?"

"Do you remember those pictures of me you took when I was still pregnant with Blaine?"

18

"How could I not?" Reaching to take out his wallet, he opened it and showed her what was kept in the clear plastic window that normally held a licence. There she was, thirty years younger, looking away from the camera, the bit of her mouth that she could see curved in a smile.

"You've kept that there all this time?"

"Of course, I did. You were my heart, Cordellia. A heart doesn't stop beating just because you can't find it anymore."

When the waitress came, she let out a happy squeal. "Why Joe! You brought a date! How fabulous! Who is the lucky lady?"

"Annie, this is Cordellia. She's a woman I loved a long time ago."

"Not the same woman that you've been pining for all these years?"

"The very same."

"Well, will wonders never cease?" She gave Cordellia a thorough once-over and nodded. "You'll do. But don't you go breaking his heart again."

"I won't, he's helping me to heal mine."

"Oh posh. Your heart is already healed or else you wouldn't be here. Good for you doll, you don't let a man like this slip away. I know several ladies who will be most upset. You've got quite the catch here."

Cordellia looked at Joe and reached across the table to take his hand. "I know."

Chapter Eight

"We're so thrilled for the release of your novel!"

Nancy's publisher, Melissa Mollina, smiled at him across the table. "Thanks, honey."

"No, Clarence, I mean it." She never called him by his nickname of Nancy, saying that she found Clarence sexier. "I know we normally have to say that about every book, but I fell in love with your novel. The characters in What's Love Got to Do with It? just leap off the page. It's as if they're real!"

Nancy smiled, his heart warming his insides. "Thank you very much."

"The novel is so Russian, has anyone told you that?"

"What do you mean Russian?"

"Well, you have all these people living big lives, they all intertwine and there are happy times and horrible things happening but, somehow, they all come out in the end. Do yourself a favour and go and read Anna Karenina by Leo Tolstoy. Best Russian novel there is."

"I'll have to give it a whirl." He didn't have the heart to tell her that he'd already read it years ago. Twice.

"What drove you to write this? I know that lots of people will want to know when it's published, but what was the spark?"

"Well, the old rule: write what you know. I had dabbled in some short stories and some poems, but I was always writing. This is the first time that I followed that rule. It's actually based off real events."

"Really? Oooh, we can put that in future editions! That makes it even more of a wonderful story."

"Well, naturally I changed names and places and some

events were made up, but at the core of the novel are real people and the lives we were leading." Nancy let out a breath, "I'm actually kind of nervous about that."

"Don't be. There is always some measure of truth in a book, something of the author within their words. Armistead Maupin's novel, The Night Listener, was based off true events. Novelists do it all the time. You followed suit by writing a story around something that happened to you and around you. Nothing to feel nervous about at all." She reached across the table and patted his hand.

He blushed. "Thanks, sweetie."

"Now, I have a surprise for you. Wait here."

She left her office and he wondered what the surprise was. He wished Michael was beside him. His cell phone buzzed, and he looked at who it was. It was as if his thoughts had called out to him. "Hey, babe. I was just thinking about you."

Michael laughed. "I'm always thinking about you. How's the meeting going?"

"Good. Melissa compared What's Love Got to Do with It? to Russian literature."

"Well, Lord knows we know a lot of drama queens."

"True that. I love you."

"I love you, too. Stop by my place when the meeting is done."

"I will."

He clicked off just as Melissa came back into the room carrying a box. She set it down on the table in front of Nancy. There was a red, sparkly bow on top.

"What is this?"

"Open it and find out."

With slightly shaking hands, Nancy opened the box. What he saw took his breath away. The box was filled with several hard copies of his book. The cover featured the faces of nine people, and a word in front of each of their faces with the last two reserved for his name. Underneath it all were the words, "A Novel."

He sat back and took a breath. "Can I open one?"

Letting out a laugh, Melissa handed him a copy. "The box is yours, silly. They're your author copies and there are twenty-five in the box. Now I want you to do something for me tonight."

"Anything."

"Take that man of yours out for a drink to celebrate. You're a published author now!" She took the red bow from on top of the box and put it on top of Nancy's head. "Perfect!"

Chapter Nine

Was is possible to be too happy?

Blaine never thought he would be asking himself this question but sometimes life changes for the better. A year ago, he had been lost and miserable, painting his heart out and trying to lose himself within himself. Now, thanks to Justin, he had been found again.

It was as if Justin had reached into the black hole that had become his life for so long and led him out. He knew it hadn't only been Justin who had offered this freedom. Blaine had wanted to go, wanted to leave that darkness.

Now, here he was, in love with the most amazing man; one that completed him rather than competed with him. Too often, relationships were about who's on top and who's on bottom. There was never a fair playing field. Now, with Justin, there was no playing field, only a field filled with flowers.

Who knew he could be such a sappy romantic?

He pressed the button for the next caller. "Thank you for calling. How can I help you today?"

"I'm having a problem with the interweb again, and I need help! I can't access my new blogger!"

"Okay, ma'am, don't worry. I can help. Just tell me what you're trying to do."

"I told you before, Blaine, not to call me 'ma'am'! It's Mo!"

"Ms. Seagrave!" He hadn't spoken to her since he helped her realize a mouse went on the desk and not on the floor like a pedal. "How are you?"

"Now don't make me tell you again to stop calling me 'Ms.' or 'ma'am!' I thought we went over this before?"

He laughed into the phone. "I'm sorry, Mo. How can I

help you today?"

"Well, I'm trying to do this blogger thing and have no idea what I'm doing. I want to blog about the books I'm reading for my book club and can't make head nor tails of it."

"I can help you with that, Mo, no problem."

He wasn't supposed to take calls about this kind of thing, only billing or technical help questions. The fact is, he hated his call centre job and made a promise to himself to help anyone who sounded as if they needed it, regardless of whether or not it went against procedure. It made the job more fun that way.

He gave his special clients his personal work number, so they were always able to get through to him when they needed to.

He took Mo through the steps of creating a blog and how to post her first blog post. When it went live, he even clicked through with her, to view the post on his end. She was ecstatic.

"Oh, Blaine! You've helped this old lady once again. Thank you so much!"

"You're welcome, Mo. It was my pleasure."

"Well, pleasure or not, I can't thank you enough. Now, I hope that someday I can repay the kindness you've shown me. How are things with that mystery man of yours?"

"He's asked me to marry him."

"Well isn't that marvelous? You must be all a dither!"

Blaine smiled, feeling his cheeks redden. "Why yes, you could say that. "

"Well, you must let me celebrate in the joy! I have to meet him! Does he treat you right?"

"Yes, Mo."

"And he makes your heart beat faster at just the thought of him?"

"Yes, he does."

"Then you've found a keeper. I want to take you and him out for drinks. You talk it over with your man, and I'll call you later this week, okay?"

"It's a date." Though there were rules in place about meeting clients outside of work, there were also rules about giving them your personal number, and he had broken that already.

"Oh, you've made this old lady very happy! You go out and do something wonderful with your man, you hear?"

Chapter Ten

When Blaine walked out of the call centre, Justin was waiting for him.

Justin never failed to take Blaine's breath away. It felt like a dream come to life. Justin was the man he had waited his entire life for and had given up hope of finding him. Having found him and fallen in love with him, he now believed in the possibility of wishes coming true.

Walking up to him, Blaine pulled Justin closer and kissed him deeply, trying to communicate through that kiss everything he felt for him. Justin kissed him back just as strongly. When they broke the kiss, Blaine saw the stars dancing in Justin's eyes.

"Well hello to you, too," Justin said. "What did I do to deserve such a fabulous welcome?"

"By just being you."

"Well in that case, prepare to be turned on as I burp the alphabet and fart duck calls."

Blaine let out a laugh. "I haven't heard you burp the alphabet, but your farts sound like ducks in distress. I wonder when they're going to come flying out of there."

Justin pulled him in for another quick kiss, then took his hand as they headed towards the library. They walked in silence for a few minutes, just relishing the sounds of the city and the life around them. Blaine wondered how he had ever felt alone here with so much going on. Perhaps he had just been too preoccupied to notice.

"What are you thinking?" Justin asked.

"Just that, somehow, you've not only changed my life, but you've changed me. You've made me a better person."

"Well, I do have my skills. Didn't I tell you that I'm magic?"

"Ha ha. No, it's just that I felt so alone before, but you've made me see life as something worth living and experiencing rather than hiding from it. How is it that one person can make me see that?"

Justin thought for a moment before answering. "Perhaps because now you know how much you're worth, how valuable you are to other people. It just took someone to make you realize that."

"But I already knew I was special."

"Yes, but did you believe it? Did you love yourself?"

"No. No, I didn't."

"There you go, then."

"I'm going to be so proud to be your husband."

"And I yours."

There was another moment of silence before Justin spoke again. "There's something you need to do for me before we can get married."

Blaine nodded, "Anything."

"I want you to meet my parents."

"Okay...why are you behaving like this is a big deal?"

"Because it is. My parents haven't met any of my boyfriends before. They can be...a little difficult."

"I'd be happy to meet them."

"You probably won't say that when you actually do meet them."

"They made you, right? So they have to be pretty awesome people."

Blaine kissed Justin's hand and they kept walking. They were just coming up to the GLBT Library entrance, where they both volunteered, when the doors flew open. Romilda stood there with a frantic look on her face.

"There you are boys! Thank God!"

"Romilda, what's wrong?" Blaine went to her side immediately. She looked ready to faint.

"Oh, it's an emergency of the highest calibre. I don't know what to do!"

"Just calm down and tell us what's happened," Justin said.

"There's a man named Gaston!"

"Oh, I like the name. Tall, dark and mysterious?" Blaine asked.

"Yes, but that's not the problem!"

"What is?"

"He wants to take me out on a date!"

"Oh, my God! It's the end of the world as we know it!" Justin said. "It's a national emergency!"

Romilda smacked him on the arm. "Didn't your mother teach you to mind your elders?"

Chapter Eleven

Devon woke when he heard knocking.

He got out of bed and shuffled to the door. Opening it, he found Rebecca standing there. When she saw him, she gave him what could only be described as a look of intense frustration.

"What the fuck is wrong with you? You don't answer your phone anymore? Do you want me to use smoke signals?"

Rebecca huffed into the apartment and closed the door. "I brought you coffee, not that you deserve it with the way you've been behaving. Why are you being such a douchebag?"

"Hello to you, too, Rebecca."

"Devon, you fucking asshole, what's wrong with you?"

Giving her a dark look, Devon said, "Are you done?"

"Yep, I'm done. Come and give mam a hug." She put down the coffees and held her arms wide open. When she hugged him, she squeezed hard, almost as if to keep him together.

"Thanks, Rebecca."

His voice was muffled so she let him go and put her hands on his shoulder. "What's your number one fag hag for, sweet cheeks? Come on, sit, talk to me."

Devon nodded and walked to the living room. Rebecca saw that the place was a mess and had likely not been cleaned in the weeks since he had lost Nancy's heart.

He sat down and reached for a bottle of wine that was sitting on the coffee table. "Want some?"

"Devon, no! You smell like an outhouse already!"

"So a little bit more won't hurt."

"That does it!" Rebecca stood and took the bottle of wine,

went to the kitchen sink and poured it down the drain.

"Hey! I was only halfway through drowning my sorrows."

"You've been doing that for six weeks now, Devon! Grow the fuck up. We're going to get you cleaned up and I'm taking you out."

"I don't want to go out."

"So what, you want to sit around your apartment bemoaning the guy who got away? You were a hooker for fuck's sake, you can find anyone you want. You'd still look half decent if you ate a meal every now and again."

"Hey, I eat." He held up an empty box of pizza pockets.

"A pizza pocket does not a meal make. When was the last time you were outside?"

"Yesterday, to get the wine you just wasted."

"No, Devon, it's you who's wasted."

"I'm not drunk yet."

"I'm talking about your life! Do you want to keep doing this to yourself? Was Nancy worth this?"

"I love him, Rebecca."

"Well, as he's moved on, you better start saying you loved him."

"You can't tell me when to stop loving someone."

"No, I can't, but you got to start loving yourself, honey. This isn't good, and I'm worried about you." She came back to the living room and sat beside Devon, putting an arm around him. "So, here's what we'll do. You'll take a shower and then get dressed because I'm taking you out on the town for an actual meal and maybe a drink if you're good."

"That won't bring Nancy back."

"True, but I'm working on bringing you back. I don't give two shits about Nancy, but I give ten shits about you." She kissed his cheek. "You dig?"

Chapter Twelve

"Romilda, would you stop pacing and tell us what's going on?"

Blaine put his hands on Romilda's shoulders and tried to stop her in her tracks. She brushed them off and kept going. She was too nervous, too edgy. "I can't. If I stop, I'll explode."

"Then maybe you could tell us what's going on?" Justin said.

"What else could be going on? There's a man whose shown interest in me, and Cordellia asked for a divorce! I don't know what to do!"

"Wait, what?" Blaine said. "How about you start with the man? That sounds interesting."

Romilda turned and faced them. She started twisting her hands. "It's a man I met a few months ago. Gaston."

"Oooh, a Frenchman. Well you know what they say," Justin said, wiggling his eyebrows.

"No, I don't know what they say!" Romilda responded, trying to keep her voice under control but losing the battle.

"Well, they're supposed to be very good in bed," he responded. "Why is this such a big deal?"

"I'm attracted to him!"

"Oh, I now see why this is a national emergency. Call the brigade!" Blaine said.

"Will you two stop making fun of me and help me figure out what to do?"

"It's simple. Do you like him?" Blaine asked.

"Yes."

"Then what's the problem?"

"He doesn't know what I am!" She said.

"Fabulous? A great dresser? Beautiful, funny, honourable?" Justin asked.

"He doesn't know that I'm trans!" she said in exasperation. "He has no idea!"

"So, tell him," Blaine said. "It's that simple."

"What if he runs away, or gets violent? That would be enough to frighten a lot of people."

"If he runs, he's not the man for you. I don't think he'll do that, though."

"He's the first man to show any sort of attraction to me as a woman."

"I don't think that's true," Justin said. "You haven't seen how the lesbians look at you, nor have you seen the other straight men in here giving you the eye."

"Only because I'm old and freakish."

"Romilda," Blaine took her hands in his. "You have to love yourself. You went through the process of becoming who you were supposed to be, right? That had to show quite a bit of self-love. So, continue that and approach the world with confidence. You're a brave woman with a good head on your shoulders. You'd be a catch for any man. Just go for a coffee or a glass of wine and see what happens. All you have to do is say 'yes.'"

Romilda calmed down and gave a watery smile. "Thanks boys. Truth be told, that's not what has me so upset. It's frightening, but I'm brave. I'll face this head on."

"You're upset about Cordellia asking for a divorce," Blaine said.

"I'm just being silly, I guess."

"No, you're not. You spent most of your life married to her. Now she's asking for a new start, a new beginning. That's got to be frightening."

"She wants to start her life again with the man she always loved. Why am I afraid of letting her go?"

"You won't let her go. Not completely. You don't just have her, you have a bond that has stretched across decades. That's not going to go away in the blink of an eye. You're friends for life."

Wiping away a tear, Romilda hugged Blaine. "I'm sorry I wasn't around to see you grow into the man you are today."

"Well, now you're around to help me continue to grow. So, don't sweat it, okay?"

She let out a nervous laugh, "Okay."

"Hey, why don't we go out for drinks after our shift and invite Gaston? I'd like to meet him, and I know that Blaine would."

"I don't have his number. He just lives in my building."

"I don't think you'll need his number," Justin said.

"Why is that?"

"Because, unless I'm mistaken, he's standing outside the front door of the library."

Romilda turned around and looked through the windows of the front doors. Standing there, wearing a grin that melted her heart, was Gaston.

Chapter Thirteen

Her legs shaking, Romilda walked towards the doors and opened them.

"Gaston! What are you doing here?"

"Well, I was walking by, going to the store next door, when I saw you come out and go back in. I figured I'd stop in and say 'hello,' see if you had given any thought to going out for a drink with me."

His smile made her believe in simple miracles. Romilda took his hand and looked into his eyes. "Gaston, there's something I have to tell you."

"Aren't you going to invite me in? I've always wanted to see this place. There are always people going in and out. I've always wondered what a gay library would offer. Is it just books about being happy?"

Romilda let out a bark of a laugh. "Oh, Gaston. It's so much more than that."

"I'm just yanking your chain. I know what GLBTQ stands for. My aunt Claire is a lesbian and proud of it. I just wanted to get that serious look off your face; you look fit to be tied."

"Not yet, she might ask for that later, though."

Romilda turned and Blaine was behind her, grinning ear to ear. He held out his hand to Gaston. "Hi there, I'm Romilda's son. Let him come in, Romilda, you look like you're guarding the place from the oncoming horde."

Gaston took Blaine's hand and gave it a good firm shake. "Nice to meet you. She didn't mention she had a son."

"She didn't know, so it's not her fault," Blaine said. "Come on in and get comfy."

Gaston followed Blaine and Romilda into the library.

Romilda thought she would choke on her heart, it was beating so fast. "Gaston, there's something I need to talk to you about."

"Well, I already know about your son, so what else is there?"

"Well, there's a reason I run this library."

"I never got the lesbian vibe off you if that's what you're getting at. If you were gay, why didn't you just say so?"

Trying to keep in a laugh, Blaine said, "I'll leave you two alone."

When he left, there was just the two of them. Other patrons milled around, looking for books, but it was as if the only person who existed for Romilda was Gaston.

"I'm not a lesbian."

"I kind of figured that," Gaston said. "I know you're attracted to me. Are you just playing hard to get?"

"No, not at all. I want you very much."

"Then what's the problem?"

"The reason I run this place is because I want to give back to the community somehow."

"That's kind of you."

"My community Gaston... Gods, there's no easy way to say this. I'm transgender, I used to live as a man. I'm so sorry." She wrung her hands and looked away from him, waiting for the inevitable. It was always this way.

Gaston was quiet for a moment then pulled chin up so that he could look at her. She almost shied away, but when he looked right into her eyes, she could see only warmth.

"Why are you sorry?" Gaston asked.

"What?"

"Why are you sorry? You have nothing to be sorry for. I didn't know you as before, I only know you as Romy, my beautiful Romy. So, why are you sorry?"

Chapter Fourteen

William wondered if wanting a drink so early in the morning made him an alcoholic.

He thought so, but if he was using alcohol to heal himself, did that make him an alcoholic or a holistic healer? Or, just full of bullshit?

He thought it was a bit of column A and a lot of column B.

When his cell phone rang again, he wanted to throw it across the room. He looked at the number on the screen. It was David.

A shiver went down his spine. On one hand, if he answered, he would be treated like crap, which would continue this evening if he got together with him. On the other hand, if he didn't answer, he would live to regret it.

He knew it was just easier to answer the phone, get it over with. "Hello?"

"Why did it ring three times? I told you to pick my calls up after one ring."

"What if I was doing something else?"

"Do you think I care? I don't like to be kept waiting. You know that. We've been through this before. Or, do you not remember the last lesson I had to teach you?"

David called them 'lessons.' They were meant to teach him how to do things the right way (David's way), how to learn to be a good boyfriend. Truth was, he was only a piece of meat to David, just another tool. David took and took but didn't give back. That was David's way.

"I'm sorry, David."

"You don't sound sorry."

"I am sorry." Sorry that I ever took up with you in the first place, William thought."I'll make you sorry. Why do you do this when you know it pisses me off?"

"God, what's your problem? You're so fucking angry. Why can't you leave a message like normal people?"

"Because I'm not normal."

"My thoughts exactly." Shit, he had meant to think that part, not say it out loud.

"What did you say to me?"

"I'm sorry."

"I'll make you sorry, that's for sure. You be at your apartment, waiting for me. I'll be there in twenty minutes. I have to teach you a lesson."

The phone cut off and William was left staring at the screen. David sounded pissed off. William knew that David's temper had nothing to do with him, that he was just permanently angry. William had tried to work past the walls that David had put up, had tried to find the person behind them, but to no avail.

Something snapped in him then. He moved without thinking. He grabbed his wallet, his phone, a charger, and a book and went to the bedroom. He threw that all into a bag with a change of clothes and some toiletries.

He wasn't going to be here when David arrived. He was going to go to the only person that could help him.

William hoped that Michael was home…and that he would talk to him.

Chapter Fifteen

"Wait, are you saying you're okay with everything?"

Romilda was having difficulty wrapping her head about this. It wasn't supposed to be so easy. There was supposed to be shock, dismay, horror, or even disgust. She wasn't used to acceptance.

"Of course, I'm okay with it. You're a woman and I'm attracted to you. What else is there?"

Letting out a breath, Romilda smiled and laughed a little. The laugh was fake, but she often used it as a way to break tension, though there was none in the air around her. "Don't you have any questions about why? I mean, most men I tell run away screaming. One of them called me unnatural."

Reaching up with his right hand, Gaston brushed his hand along her face. She was amazed at the shiver that ran through her body. She hadn't felt like this in years. If he kept touching her, she would melt right there on the library floor.

"They weren't real men then."

She shook her head. "How can you be so accepting?"

"How can you not be?"

That made Romilda catch her breath. "What do you mean?"

"Well, babe, it's like you're looking for a fight, or you're put off because I'm not running for the hills or something."

"No! Why would I do that?"

"Well, you've spent an awful long time trying to convince me I'm not worth your time. There must be some reason why you feel that way."

"I just don't know what you want from me."

"I want you to love me, eventually," he said quietly. "But

first, you gotta work on loving yourself."

There was a noise behind them. Romilda turned and saw Justin standing there. "I'm sorry to interrupt but you're both blocking the door."

She turned the other way to see a few patrons waiting to come in to the library. Blushing, Romilda moved out of the way and Gaston did the same.

Turning back to her, Gaston took her hands in his. "Just promise you'll let me take you out for a drink tonight. Just one drink, that's all I ask."

Romilda let out a shaky breath and nodded, her heart beating loudly inside of her. "All right. One drink."

"I'll pick you up at seven? I know a nice place, really classy, just like you."

He leaned forward to kiss her hand and she let him, revelling in the heat that ran up her arm. Gaston gave her one more smile and then he was gone.

"What have I just done?" she asked.

Beside her, Justin let out a long sigh. "Honey, you better snap him up, or I will."

Romilda slapped his hand. "You're practically married."

"I might be practically married, but I'm not dead, and I know a good man when I see one. So should you."

Chapter Sixteen

Rebecca sometimes wondered what it would have been like if her life had been different. Would she have married Devon? Would they have had children? Maybe instead of thinking about what her life would have been like, she wondered why she had ever been in love with him when she damn well knew that Devon was gay.

She had always known that it was a one-sided love affair—he wouldn't and couldn't love her back. Even before he came out of the closet, she knew he was gay. She had a very good gaydar, for a straight woman.

From afar, she had watched as he entered one failed relationship after another. Part of it was because the guys had been douchebags, but another part was because he was emotionally unavailable. Being a hooker kind of did that to you.

Now, here she was, staring at him as he got ready to go out. Rebecca watched as he picked out his pants, shirt, and shoes with such precision that it broke her heart. She wanted to wrap him up in a hug and never let him go. Instead, she had to play it cool, knowing he could never love her back in that way.

"For fuck's sake, Dev. You're not getting ready for a job interview. We're going out for a drink or two. What would you normally wear to a bar?"

He looked lost. He stood there holding his fancy dress shoes and a jar of polish. "I don't know. I was always working in one or hooking in one. I haven't been to one just to hang out with no purpose for years now."

"Well, what would you wear if we were going to hang out

at one?"

"We are going to hang out at one."

"Focus Dev, focus. What would you wear to relax, to just have a good time?"

"I don't know what a good time is anymore."

"Oh, for fuck's sake."

Rebecca poured them each a glass of sparkling water and steered him towards his bedroom. She had a fleeting flash of him naked on the bed, waiting for her. She gave her head a shake to clear that thought and went to his closet instead.

Going to his closet, she picked out a green hoodie and dark blue jeans. After that, she went to his dresser and pulled out a light grey t-shirt. "There, your outfit for the evening has been chosen."

"I've had those clothes for ages. Why would you pick that?"

"Are you trying to meet someone or impress them?"

"A little of both, I guess."

"Then be yourself. You're impressive enough as it is. Besides, if you wear something super fancy, you'll be too focused on what you're wearing and not who you're with."

His smile lit her heart aflame. "What would I do without you?"

"Starve and walk around looking like crap all the time."

"Why did you pick those clothes?"

"I just know what you look good in, that's all. Now go and shower."

Rebecca could never tell him that the outfit she picked for him was what he had been wearing the first time she had met him. She would remember that day forever.

Holy fuck, she needed to get laid.

Chapter Seventeen

Nancy was cooking dinner. This in itself was something of a miracle.

"What are you doing?" Mike asked.

"I thought I was making dinner for my man. Why, is this not how you're supposed to do it?" Nancy grinned at him and held out a spatula. "Pour me a drink, handsome. Wine's over there."

"What are we having? I didn't even know you could cook."

"My mama wouldn't have set me loose in the world without knowing a few things in the kitchen."

"Like where to keep the booze and chocolate?"

"Smart ass. Everyone knows white goes in the fridge and red goes on the counter and the chocolate is already gone. However, I love you, so you're forgiven."

"I'm honoured. How come you've never cooked for me before?"

"I have to keep some things a mystery, don't I? Can't reveal all of my secret talents before we're living together."

"I certainly hope some of those secret talents extend to the bedroom."

"Oh honey, you know it. Tonight, however, is all about celebration. I'm making us some salmon steaks and a salad. I got red wine though, hope that's okay."

"What's the occasion?"

"Well, my publisher told me to take you out to dinner. I decided to do this at home because you can't get naked at a restaurant."

Michael wrapped his arms around Nancy and kissed his neck. "No, that's kind of frowned upon."

"So, you see my point."

"I do. What are we celebrating?"

"Look on the table. I've autographed a copy for you."

Mike approached the dining room table and saw a book waiting there for him. He knew its title already, having read the entirety of Nancy's manuscript. But somehow seeing it on the cover of a book took his breath away.

"Open to the title page," Nancy said from the kitchen.

On the title page was an inscription that read:

Michael.

You've changed my life and made me a better man.

My life would not be complete without you.

All my love,

Nancy

Tears came to Michael's eyes and he was surprised, as he was every time, at how much he loved Nancy. It never failed to leave him breathless.

"Now, turn to the dedication."

Mike did so and saw the following:

For Michael, who proved that love was a possibility instead of a dream.

Now he was full-out crying. He went back to the kitchen, still holding the book, and crushed Nancy to him, kissing him with everything he had. He tried to communicate how much he loved him in that kiss, how every moment he spent with him, he fell even more in love.

Nancy pulled away. "Babe, I love you, but my book is crushing into my back."

Mike laughed. "Sorry about that. I just can't help myself around you. I love you so much, you know that, right?"

"Of course, I do." He handed Mike a glass of wine. "Now, cheers honey!"

They clinked glasses together at the exact moment the doorbell rang.

Chapter Eighteen

Nancy turned to look at the door. The person knocked again. He got a bad feeling in his stomach and put his hand out to Michael. "Don't answer. Whoever it is will go away."

The knocking became louder and Nancy felt sure that he could see the door wobbling. Old houses weren't meant to live up to such abuse. Michael seemed to read his mind.

"I don't know if the door can take much more of that."

"They'll go away. They just have to."

"Why don't we just open it?" Michael asked. "It can't be that bad, can it?"

A voice yelled at them through the door. It sounded heartsick and broken. "Michael! Mikey, I know you're in there! I can hear you talking! Answer the door!"

Michael went pale. "It's William."

Nancy let out a soft chuckle that had no humour in it. "I could have told you that much. You stay there."

"What are you doing?"

"Bitch thinks he can try to knock down my door to get to you? He doesn't know who he's messing with here. I'm not some hussy that's going to hide."

Nancy stomped to the front door and pulled it wide open...just as William went to knock on the door again. Instead of knocking on the door, he ended up hitting Nancy in the face. The blow sounded like a canon going off, the bones of William's knuckles hitting the bones of Nancy's nose.

"Motherfucker!" Nancy screamed. He backed away from William, holding his nose.

William went from enraged to apologetic in a millisecond. "Oh, God, Nancy, I'm so freaking sorry!"

He moved to come in, but Nancy held up his other hand. "Oh, hell no. If you think you're coming in here, you have another thing coming."

"Please, just let me talk to Michael. I'm in trouble, and only he can help me."

"Funny, I don't remember Mike helping you before; it was some old fucker in the washroom, right?"

"Please! Michael!" He was screaming now and tearing at his hair. "Please, you gotta help me! I don't know what to do!"

Michael came up behind Nancy and put a hand on his shoulder. "Let him in. It'll be better than him standing on the front porch screaming his head off."

Nancy looked at Michael, fire burning in his eyes. "Okay, but only because I want to."

"Thank you." Mike kissed him softly on the lips and they heard William let out a strangled cry.

"Does he make you happy, Michael? Does he really? I know they say that black men have big cocks, but there's more than that to love."

"Get the fuck in here."

Michael pulled him into the house and closed the door. "How did you know where to find me, anyway? I haven't talked to you in weeks."

"Where else would you go but your love nest?" He let out another cry. "Ours is so empty without you there."

"Yeah, well you made your bed, you fucking lie in it," Nancy spat at him.

Mike touched Nancy's lips with one finger to quiet him. "Only a couple more minutes, okay?"

"Okay."

Mike turned to William. "What's the real problem? I've never seen you so riled up."

"It's David. He's fucking crazy."

"Well, we already know that. Look at what he did to Blaine and to Devon. What's he got to do with you?" Nancy asked him.

"I'm with him. I mean, we're fucking, and I thought I could deal with him at first, but he's become so controlling and awful. I was just so messed up when you left me, Michael."

"Oh, no you don't!" Nancy said. "Don't you dare pin your choices on Mike. Those were your decisions, not his."

"He beats me."

William said this so quietly, so softly, that Nancy wasn't sure he had heard at first. "What's that? What did you say?"

"He beats me. He beats me, and I don't know what to do."

With that, William burst into tears and covered his face with his hands. Nancy looked at Mike, wondering what they were going to do.

Chapter Nineteen

She had to do something about this. The stress wasn't good for the baby.

Poppy had to know why Dava wouldn't marry her. Not that marriage was the point anymore. More, it was the fact that Dava hid something from her. It was eating away at Poppy. She wished she had someone to talk to.

When the light bulb went off, it was blinding. She couldn't believe that it had taken this long to think of Blaine. What was the point of having a gay best friend if you couldn't call on him in times of need?

She threw some things in a bag and went to the elevator to go up to Blaine's apartment. It had become a little bit of a love nest since Justin had proposed. Not that she wasn't happy for her bestie or anything, but still. There was only so much lovey-dovey stuff she could take before she threw up.

Poppy got on the elevator and, as the doors closed, her cell phone rang. Looking at the screen, she saw it was Blaine. She answered, "Well if it isn't my FGBF!"

"What's an FGBF?"

"My Fabulous Gay Best Friend! Do you like it? I'm going to make the internet go wild with it once I hashtag it all over the place."

"How much wine have you had tonight, sweetie?"

"None and that's part of the problem."

"What are you doing tonight? Justin and I wanted to take you out to dinner somewhere nice. Are you doing anything with Dava? She could come with us if you'd like."

"Oh, shit honey, I'm heading somewhere right now, actually." Poppy got out of the elevator and walked down the hallway.

"Well, maybe you can stop by when you're done whatever you're doing? I don't see you enough, and it's been far too long."

"Sorry sweet cheeks, I really wish I could." She knocked on the door.

"I wish you could, too. Sorry, someone just knocked on the door."

Poppy knocked again, waited a few seconds and knocked once more. "You better answer that. It sounds urgent."

"Sorry honey, this won't take long. Wait there, okay?"

"No problem."

When the door opened, Blaine's face was tense for a moment but relaxed into a big and beautiful smile the moment he saw her. "Poppy!" He threw his arms around her. "Why you little minx! What are you doing here? I thought you had to go somewhere."

She looked at him. "Blaine, it's a gosh darn good thing you're so good looking. It makes up for your blonde moments."

Poppy sailed into the apartment and Blaine closed the door behind her. "Hey, I resemble the remark. Did you want anything to drink?"

"I got that covered, sweetie. What kind of mocktail do you want?" She opened her bag and pulled out two bottles. "I got fake cosmos or fake margaritas."

"I think I'll make myself a real cosmo, actually."

"Sure, make the pregnant woman suffer. Where's your lover boy?"

"Out picking up a pizza."

"I hope there's enough for me. "

"He's getting a large. I'll call him and ask him to pick up

two, one for us and one for you."

"Ha ha, you're so funny. But in all seriousness, thank you."

"What's up honey? Are you okay?"

"Oh, I'm good. I think Dava is cheating on me. How have things been with you?"

Chapter Twenty

Cordellia was astonished to realize she was happy.

It was such an odd emotion for her that she didn't know what she was feeling at first, but as she walked down First Avenue, hand in hand with Joe, she realized that the only thing it could be was happiness.

Cordellia had spent years in self-induced misery: the break-up of her marriage, her former husband's subsequent gender transition, hiding who she really was from Blaine all the time; all while watching Blaine try again and again to find love when she was too afraid to do so.

"I'm no longer afraid," Cordellia said.

"Well, that's a good thing. Though my hair is rather frightening when I get out of bed in the morning," Joe said.

"Oh, Joe. Everyone's is."

"So then, what are you no longer afraid of?"

"Lots of things. Of living life, being myself, and being proud to be who I am and the life I've led."

"Well, that life did lead you to me, so that's pretty amazing."

"Can you forgive me?"

"We've been through this, Cordellia."

"We have, but hear me out, okay? I want to apologize to you over and over again until I'm blue in the face. I only have one regret in this life, and that's what I did to you."

"You did what you had to do. There's no shame in that."

"I left you with no explanation. How can you be so accepting?"

Joe stopped walking and took both of her hands in his. "When you love someone, that's just what you do. Life is too

51

short to hold on to things that hurt you."

Cordellia let out a laugh. "I wish I'd figured that out while I was trying to hold to Ernest."

"You were only doing what you thought was right. You can't be so hard on yourself for your past. Just embrace the future and live for that, instead of reliving what was."

She was filled with love for this man who had held her heart for so long. "Thank you."

"For what?"

"For loving me all of these years, instead of growing to hate me. A lot of men would have."

"I'm not most men."

"I've noticed."

Leaning forward, Cordellia pressed her lips softly against Joe's. It was hesitant at first, but as the heat grew between them, they kissed in earnest. Cordellia tried to let her kiss tell him how much she loved him. She knew that there were some thing that could never be truly communicated with words.

Joe put his arms around her and kissed her even more deeply, as if he were trying to do the same. It felt like the first time, but it also spoke of a history between them that didn't need words.

When she broke the kiss, it was to find Joe staring at her, tears streaming down his face. She touched a finger to one of them. "What's wrong?"

"Nothing, except that I'm so incredibly happy. It's like you've given me my life back."

"And we can work on building a new future together. We're only in our sixties. That's two more decades, more if they figure out how to stop the aging process." She smiled at him jokingly.

A shadow of something passed over his face. His smile

faltered for a millisecond, then was gone. "Of course." He kissed her again, more urgently and heated with words left unsaid.

She touched his face, wiping away a few more of the tears. "Would you spend the night with me?"

A genuine smile filled his face with light. "Honey, I would be delighted."

Chapter Twenty-One

"So, what makes you think Dava is having an affair?" Blaine asked.

He tried to keep his voice calm, knowing Poppy always went to the most dramatic reasoning. She was like a gay man that way, always in love with the drama. However, that was the last thing she needed right now.

"I asked her to marry me and she said no."

"What?"

"Well, not no, not really. She said that we should just enjoy each other's company…"

"Why do I hear a 'but' there?"

"Because there is. I told her that I didn't want to raise this baby alone, that it meant a lot to me to have two parents instead of one."

"What?" Blaine said again. "That's really status quo of you."

"I know, it surprised me, too. You wouldn't think I would go all in for the picture of the perfect family, but there you are."

"Well colour me surprised."

"I'd rather colour you pink—it's more you."

"Focus, Poppy, focus."

"Right, so I just can't get over the feeling that she's hiding something. She was so evasive, and I can't think of why she wouldn't want to get married. I mean, doesn't she want me?"

"Poppy, you know she does. Dava is crazy about you!"

Her eyes started to water. "Then why doesn't she want me?"

"Oh honey…" He sat down beside her on the couch, taking her drink and putting both of them on the coffee table.

"You know you won't have to raise this baby alone, don't you?"

"How so, if Dava won't have me as a wife?"

"Well, Justin is the father. He's going to be a huge part of this baby's life. He's already started buying toys in purple because you don't know the gender yet. And I'm going to be the best uncle ever. I've already started buying lots of books; you can never start too early. Nancy will make a great aunt, and Nan is all ready to be a grandmother. You won't be alone."

The tears flowed freely from Poppy's eyes now. Somehow they made her look more beautiful. "God, I wish you weren't gay Blaine."

"I am and so are you."

"Yeah, but I can always dream, right? How do you always know how to say the right thing?"

Instead of replying, he drew her in to a big hug, wrapping his arms around her and holding her close. Poppy sighed in contentment and nuzzled against him. "Can I spend the night here? I don't want to be alone."

"I wouldn't have it any other way," Blaine whispered.

There was a noise at the door and Justin walked in, carrying two large pizzas. The aroma of cheese and sauce and meat filled the air as Justin brought them into the living room. "I got two larges. I figured if we were having a pregnant houseguest, we'd need more than one pizza," he said with a smile.

"Bitch!" Poppy retorted.

"Hussy," Justin shot back. "How are you, sweetie?"

She looked at Blaine, then at Justin. "I'm much better now." Poppy got up and gave him a kiss on the cheek. "So, are we going to sit here just smelling the food, or are we going to eat it? I'm starving!"

Chapter Twenty-Two

Sebastian wondered why it had taken so long to get his stuff in order.

His life had begun again once he started to accept himself, so the time before wasn't in question. Since he transitioned, he had been in one disastrous relationship after another and had just stopped trying. Until Chuck.

Normally, Chuck would not have been his type at all. The jock guy, always looking to put their cock in someone else, turned Sebastian off. But there was just something endearing and wonderful about Chuck that sent his heart aflutter.

Looking around their new apartment, he was filled with a sense of glee, of happiness that he had never had before. They were building something here, something wonderful. The move had gone well, and they hadn't killed each other. Always a good sign.

He couldn't wait to start building a new life with Chuck, the man of his dreams. It just goes to show that it's never the person we think it will be who catches our heart. That person always comes out of left field and hits a home run.

Clearly, he had been around Chuck long enough if he was already starting to think in sports analogies, but that was all right. He might like baseball and football, but everyone had their faults.

Chuck came into the room and took in the mountains of boxes. He whistled. "Man, you look happy for someone surrounded by a bunch of stuff. We have a lot of work ahead of us."

"Of course, I'm smiling. We get to build our home together, isn't that awesome?"

Grinning, Chuck stepped over a few boxes and wrapped his arms around him. "Yes, it is. I never thought this would happen, not in a million years. I'm so glad that it's with you."

"Do you feel like pizza tonight or Chinese? I say we do take-out and beer."

"Oh, no. We can't have beer here on our first night. I have something I've put aside for a night like this."

Sebastian went to the cooler that he had filled with all the food from his fridge. He opened it to reveal a large bottle of champagne.

"You can't have champagne with pizza."

"Who says?"

"Me. Pizza goes with beer."

"Are you sure you're gay? Pizza and beer is such a straight-guy meal."

"You tell me, you've had my cock in your mouth."

Letting out a laugh, Sebastian kissed him. "Too true. Okay, pizza and beer it is. We can save the champagne for later tonight. Let's get a couple of the boxes done and then order the food."

His cell phone rang. Looking down at the call display, Sebastian saw a number that sent chills down his spine. Knowing he shouldn't answer, knowing that he would regret answering, his finger hit the accept button anyways.

"Hello handsome," a breathy woman's voice said.

"Listen to me. I don't know how you got this number, but you need to lose it right now. Do you hear me? Never call me again!"

He hit the end call button and dropped his phone on the counter with a bang. Turning, he saw Chuck looking at him with shock.

"How about that beer?" Sebastian said.

Chapter Twenty-Three

"Okay, I'm ready."

Devon couldn't believe he was doing this. He would much rather stay indoors in his apartment with all the lights off, contemplating how he had fucked up. He really knew how to live.

He had never been so affected by another man before. Usually, he was too busy looking for his next hook-up, so he could score his next hit of cash. Meeting Nancy had thrown him off kilter. He thought it would be fun, a little sweaty roll around. He had not planned on falling in love with Nancy. That had caught them both by surprise.

The difference was that Nancy was willing to do almost anything for love. Devon was only willing to keep doing whatever he wanted and had expected Nancy to be okay with that. Devon knew now that he hadn't valued Nancy enough or cherished the love that was given him.

Devon had tried to win him again with flowers, chocolates, jewellery, and CDs. Nancy had sent it all back to him unopened. As a last attempt, Devon had shipped Nancy a new leather coat. Nancy had returned it with a note: Stop trying to buy the love that is no longer yours.

After that, the depression had taken hold. He had become lost within himself, not wanting to find his way out again. He had quit hooking and stopped engaging with the life outside of his apartment door. The fact that a man was doing this to him drove him even crazier. He tried to convince himself that Nancy was just a femme, a fairy fag, and not worth his time. However, Devon knew the argument was invalid.

Thinking of all this while he stared at himself in the

mirror, he sighed.

"For goodness sake. We're going out to party. The least you could do is look happy about it," Rebecca snapped.

Devon turned to face her. "I'm sorry, honey."

"We're just going out to have fun, Devon. You don't have to look like I'm dragging you off to a firing range for an execution. I don't have to do this, you know."

"I know, hon, I'm sorry. I'm just down."

"Well, we're trying to get you up. In more ways than one."

"Ew."

"Seriously, what if you meet a nice guy?"

"Rebecca, I'm still in mourning. The last thing I want to do is meet a man."

"Then let's get you laid. Hopefully, if you get blood running down in the nether regions, it won't fall off from lack of use."

"Bitch."

"Hag. Now grab your coat and let's go."

Devon just stood there for a moment. He was silent for a minute but finally asked the questions he had been holding in, "What if I run into guys that I used to fuck for money?"

"So, what if you do? They all wanted you then, and they'll still want you now. At the very least, you'll get a few free drinks out of it."

"What if the guys there know about Nancy and me?"

"This community is small, so they will know. But they will also know you're free and single now, so it's all good to be out on the town."

Then Devon quietly asked the question he had been most afraid to voice, "What if no one likes me?"

"Oh, honey." Rebecca came to him and drew him into her arms. She ran her fingers through his hair. "That's okay if no one does, because I love you. If they don't see how fabulous you are, who needs them?"

She held him close for a few minutes before stepping away. "Ready to go now? Let's go kick some dance-floor ass."

Devon nodded and pretended not to notice the tears at the corners of her eyes.

Chapter Twenty-Four

The place was hopping. They could hear melodious music with a loud beat thumping through the windows. People were standing outside smoking their cigarettes, and it looked like fog in the night air.

As Devon walked up the street with her, Rebecca took his hand and gave it a squeeze. "Don't look so frightened. They won't bite unless you ask them to."

"I won't be the one doing the asking."

"If you find the right guy you will."

"Yeah, right."

"Have a little faith in yourself. You're hot, you got a smoking body and a brain to boot. What's not to like? Now come on, let's get some drinks and loosen up a little."

"Okay, but just one."

"God, I can't believe the straight woman is trying to corrupt the gay guy. You should be leading me downhill to sin, not the other way around."

He gave her an incredulous look. "You forget I know you."

"Touché. Come on, the music is going, and the drinks are flowing."

Hooking her arm in his, they made their way to the front steps of the bar, past the people gathered there and into the half-lit interior. People always looked amazing in bars, Rebecca thought. It was all down to the lighting. Then you get them home, and in the morning you realize you'd slept with Quasimodo. It had happened to her more times than she could count.

It was a newer bar. Devon hadn't wanted to go to The Cabin and Rebecca couldn't blame him. The place was a dump. This place was called Groove and it was for gays and straights alike. She sure as fuck hoped that some guy here would find Devon attractive, even though the thought of that broke her heart a little.

Rebecca knew that the chances of her finding love were few and far between, especially when her heart belonged to him. Still, a roll in the hay would be fun. It had been quite a while since she had last had a good ride.

Ordering two drinks, a cosmo for her and a mojito for Devon, she led him to the dance floor. She could hear the music and it was louder there. Sometimes, she liked to come to these places alone and just lose herself in the music. She could forget who she was and the secrets she carried.

She glanced at Devon and was thrilled to see a bit of life coming back into his face. She leaned in close to him and could smell his scent, an earthy fragrance of sandalwood, except deeper somehow. "You got this." She scanned the dance floor. "Look, that guy is already checking you out."

Rebecca used her chin to point towards a tall man with black hair that was looking at Devon in shock. He had black spiky hair, just as Devon did and a gorgeous amount of stubble covered his chin. "Go on, he looks like he wants you already."

"No, I don't think that will work."

"Why not? He's hot, doesn't look like he's here with anyone. What's the problem?"

"The problem is that he's my brother. I know Rocky Horror implied that incest was best and to keep it in the family, but I just don't swing that way."

Chapter Twenty-Five

"Your brother? You never said you had a brother."

"We don't get along very well."

"Your parents must have loved having two gay sons."

"Yes, except they didn't. It was just me. Dylan is straight."

Looking at Dylan from across the room, she could see the family resemblance. The same dark hair and dark eyes that Devon had, the same strong chin with the cleft that cried out to be kissed. As Dylan made his way over to them, Rebecca watched him move to the beat of the music. That beat was echoed by her heart. It thumped in her chest, loud and insistent. She took a deep breath and motioned to a waiter so that she could order a drink…or three.

When Dylan was in front of them, Rebecca saw that though the brothers looked similar, there were differences. There were ebony streaks in his hair and flecks in his dark brown eyes that looked like gold. His lips were also fuller and suppler. Rebecca wanted to bite them. Where was the waiter with that fucking drink?

"Hey slut!" he said.

For a moment, Rebecca thought that he was talking to her, then she realized that he was looking at Devon. "You can't talk to him that way."

"Why not, it's what he is."

"Hello to you, Dylan. So nice to see you."

"Too bad we didn't see you for Mom's birthday. What was the excuse this time? "

"I was busy."

"Fucking some other horny guy that couldn't get laid without paying for it?"

"Why are you talking to him this way?" Rebecca asked.

"Because it's who he is and what he does. Nothing matters to him more than the all mighty cock attached to the all mighty dollar."

"For your information" —she poked Dylan in the chest— "he doesn't do that anymore."

"Why not, whore face? Did you catch an STD?"

"You really are a piece of shit. You have no idea, do you?" Rebecca said. She tried to keep her voice down but wasn't very successful. "He lost the love of his life and has been depressed for weeks. But you wouldn't know that, would you? Because you're a small minded fuckwad."

Devon put his hand on her arm. "Rebecca…"

"I'm not finished. Your brother is one of the most caring, loving men I have ever known."

"You haven't met many men then, have you? Either that, or your standards are really low."

"You total asshole!" Not thinking, Rebecca grabbed a drink from the person dancing next to them and threw it in Dylan's face. His shocked expression dripped with clear liquid, and the air was filled with the scent of pine.

"Come on Devon, we're leaving." Rebecca turned around "Come on, sweetie. Let's just go."

"That's fine. I don't feel much like drinking and dancing now, anyway." He walked towards the door and Rebecca went to follow, except she felt another hand on her arm. She turned and looked from Dylan's hand to his face. Instead of looking angry, he seemed intrigued.

"What might your name be, Miss?"

She sucked in a breath and tried not to melt. "My name? It's Go Fuck Yourself."

"Well, Go Fuck Yourself, I'm pleased to meet you. I'm

Dylan."

"Yeah, I gathered that. Though I think that Asshole von Asshat suits you better."

"Anyone told you that you have a dirty mouth on you?"

"Yeah, well I haven't used it on you yet, so save your judgement until then."

"I look forward to it. Can I get your number?"

"What? I just called you an asshole and an asshat and threw a drink in your face. Why the fuck would you want my number?"

"Why? Well quite honestly, I haven't ever met anyone who stood up for my brother. You must be quite a person if you can see something in him that the rest of us can't. Aside from that, you have fire. I want to see if that flame exists in other areas as well."

Her cheeks warmed at his word. "You're quite full of yourself, aren't you?"

"Better than being full of shit."

Rebecca couldn't help herself, she laughed. "Okay asshole. Here." She took his phone and put her number in the contacts under the name of Go Fuck Yourself.

He handed Rebecca his phone and entered his number. She took her phone back and changed his name to I'm an Asshole.

With a grin, she handed Dylan's phone back to him and went in search of Devon.

Chapter Twenty-Six

Devon hated bars. He hated the whole scene, the whole fakery of it.

He was sure he had seen some of the gay guys here in all the other bars. It was always the same ones, sitting there and judging every other guy as unworthy because they didn't look the right way or didn't have the right amount of muscles. Or, maybe they couldn't smell money on you, or you weren't wearing the right clothes.

In Devon's experience, and he had a lot of it, men didn't care about the man behind the dick. They just wanted one thing and that was the wham-bam-thank-you-Stan. They didn't care about the man behind the clothes or muscles, what drove him and inspired him. The very fact that Devon was able to have such a long and fruitful career as a prostitute was proof of that.

Lighting another cigarette, Devon turned around to go ask Rebecca what was taking so long and found himself face to face with a man.

The guy had scraggly blonde hair and wore glasses with thick black frames. He had blueish-green eyes and a smile with one crooked tooth that just made it all the more endearing. He was stout, about 5'5", and perhaps twenty pounds overweight.

"Hey, sorry man. I didn't mean to disturb you."

The guy went to walk away, and Devon found himself wanting to hear his voice again. It was deeper than he thought it would be, and it had been so long since he had talked to another man. "It's okay. You weren't disturbing me."

The guy turned back to him. "That's good. You looked so serious. Far too serious for this place."

"Just thinking about how fake this all is."

"You mean the bar?"

"Yeah. How other gay men treat each other, always basing what they think of the guy based on how he looks. When was the last time you had a real conversation with another man?"

"Oh, well, does this count? This is pretty deep."

"Seriously? I'm the only one you've had a conversation with?"

"Well, I always play by my standby rule."

"What's that?"

"Nothing happens until the second date."

"What?! No kissing or anything?"

"I'm not a nun for Christ's sake. Kissing is fine, sure, but nothing below the belt."

"What happens on the second date?"

"All bets are off."

"So, when was the last time you've had a second date?"

"That's the problem. I haven't. No guy wants to get to know me before shoving their cock in my mouth. What's up with that?"

Letting out a laugh, Devon said, "You have no idea. I totally understand what you're talking about."

The guy stuck out his hand. "My name's Curtis."

"I'm Devon."

"Want to get out of here, Devon? Go and get a glass of wine somewhere quieter?"

Devon thought about saying "No thank you and nice to meet you" and walking away. However, his mouth spoke for him as his heart had other ideas. "I would love to. Just let me go find my friend Rebecca and tell her where I'm going. "

"Bring her along."

"Seriously?"

"Why not? That way you'll have someone else's opinion of me. Hey, you never know. Anything helps, right?"

Devon heard a throat clear behind him and turned to see Rebecca standing there with a smile on her face. "Hey, stud muffin. Who's your friend?"

Chapter Twenty-Seven

"Hey there. I'm Curtis."

Curtis held out his hand to Rebecca and shook it. Rebecca had to admit, he wasn't the type of guy that Devon normally went for. She glanced over at him and saw, to her surprise, that Devon looked smitten.

"Very nice to meet you Curtis. What's the haps?"

"Well, I just invited Devon here out for a drink. And you, too, of course."

"Me too?"

"Sure, the more the merrier, right? I told Devon that you could vet me. That way, I get to spend more time with this gorgeous man here and get to know one of his friends. Win-win, I'd say."

Rebecca's eyebrows rose. "No need to vet you, I'm already impressed. Where are we going?"

"A little club I like. They play soft jazz and they're open all night. Even better, they have the best wine on offer anywhere. What do you say? You both want to come with me?"

"Oh, well, if Devon doesn't want to, I'm all in."

"Okie dokie, you guys ready to go? The club is just down the street."

"Sure, let me just have a quick chat with Devon and we're all yours."

"Cool! I have to get my coat. Meet me here in five? I just have to tell the guys I came with that I'm heading out."

"Oh, we wouldn't want to take you away from your friends."

"It's all good. I have a feeling the evening will get better from here on out."

Curtis flashed a smile at Devon and went back into the bar. Rebecca turned to Devon, "So?"

"So, what?"

"Do you want to go with him?"

"More than you could know."

"Could have fooled me, you were quieter than a church lady."

"I'm so nervous! What if I fuck it up? What if I break his heart, too?"

"Devon, he wants to take you out for a drink, not declare everlasting love. Not yet anyways."

"Oh, Becca, stop! I'm nervous enough as it is!"

"You weren't nervous when you were out here alone talking to him."

"That was just talking. Now he'll want to get to know all about me."

"Oh my god! He'll want to have a conversation! Sound the alarms!"

"Be serious for a second. It's too soon after Nancy; I'm still damaged."

"No, you're not. You're hurting, sure, but that's to be expected. What better way to get over your pain than to have some fun? A handsome man wants to talk to you and you don't even have to get paid! What a notion!"

"Well, to be fair, my clients and I didn't do much in the way of talking."

"And that's part of your problem. So suck it up buttercup. We're fucking going."

Curtis returned with a smile on his face. "Ready?"

Rebecca looked at Devon. She would let him call this one. She watched him take a deep breath and let it out slowly.

"Ready, set, go," Devon said.

Chapter Twenty-Eight

Cordellia opened her eyes and realized for the first time in a long time, she was at peace.

It was a strange sensation. She had been a carrier of secrets for so long—of anguish, jealousy, even hatred. She had despised Romilda for so long over going away to become who she was meant to be, unwittingly leaving Cordillia to raise Blaine alone when she had left Joe behind.

He had been half of her heart then, and she was thrilled to have it back.

Arms wrapped around her and pulled her close. Joe's voice spoke into her ear, "Morning gorgeous. How'd you sleep?"

"Better than I have in a long time. Though I will probably be sore today. You sure know how to give an old lady a workout."

"Honey, you were the one giving me the workout, and there's nothing old about you. At least not in here." Joe touched her where her heart sat inside of her chest. "Nothing old at all."

"How can you say that when I'm covered with wrinkles? I look like a map to the London subways or something."

"No, those are experience lines, not wrinkles. They make you even more beautiful."

"Oh, you old flirt!"

"No, it's true. See, this line..." He traced a finger along her jaw. "This was when you learned to speak out loud what your heart wanted. This line…" He drew a finger down her neck to the top of her breasts. "This was when you held Blaine to you for the first time and forged a bond that would never die. This line…" He drew a finger down along her left breast, right over her heart. "This was when you said you loved me for the first time."

Warmth ran though Cordellia and she snuggled closer to Joe, pulling his arms tighter around her. "Why did I take so long to get back to you?"

"You had to wait until you were ready. That's all there is to it. It wouldn't have felt right otherwise."

They were silent for a moment, each taking comfort in the sound of the others breathing. Then Cordellia said, "Thank you."

"For what?"

"For just being yourself. For finding romance in the most normal things. For making me feel things I haven't felt in a long time, even though I always held a spark for you that I would hope one day ignite into a flame."

"You know I feel the same, right?" Joe asked.

"Of course I do."

"And nothing would hurt me more than to hurt you."

"I know that, Joe. What's wrong? Is there something the matter?"

"Nothing, nothing is the matter anymore. Let's just enjoy the time we have together and revel in it. Okay?"

Cordellia nodded and snuggled closer against him but couldn't escape the notion that he had avoided mentioning something. She knew whatever it was, he would tell her in time. It still made her wonder, though.

Joe had never kept anything from her before. What was he hiding now?

Chapter Twenty-Nine

Nancy woke with a kink in his neck. Named William.

It had been odd having him spend the night. Mostly, they just sat there and let William cry it out. After his declaration of what David did to him, he said no more. Instead, he moped around the flat, drank a lot of their booze, then passed out.

Michael stood with his arms wrapped around Nancy. They both looked down at William. He lay on the floor with his coat as a pillow and his pants covering him partially, like a blanket. "Shouldn't we have moved him to the couch or something?"

"Oh, honey, why? After what he put you through?"

"Yeah, but you know I'm still legally married to him, right?"

"Honey, that doesn't make him our responsibility."

"Then what do we do with him? We can't let him go back out there where David will be waiting for him."

"Well, we can't keep him here. There's not enough room. This is supposed to be our home. He's the one who's crashing."

"What's wrong with you? Can't you see he's in pain? We have to do something."

"Fine. Call the police and put a 'return to sender' sticker on him."

"Nancy."

Nancy turned to Mike when he heard the tone of his voice. "I'm sorry, I didn't sleep well last night and I'm being a bitch. I like William, I really do. I just don't like what he did to you and I'm kind of biased. I just don't want him hurting you again."

"So, what do we do? Where can he go? I mean, when

David was after Blaine, he found him everywhere he went. We can't let William deal with that. Not in his state."

"He needs somewhere safe to go, somewhere where David won't think to go."

"He needs someone to look after him, too," Michael said.

A light bulb went off in Nancy's head. Michael loved the way that his eyes lit up when Nancy got a really good idea. "We can have Cordellia look after him!"

"Cordellia? I don't know. She's got her own shit going on, and he'd be a handful."

Nancy's face was still animated. "No, she loves looking after people. It brings out her motherly instincts."

"Yeah, but does she know him that well? Won't that be odd?"

"How about instead of trying to ship me off somewhere, you ask me what I'd like to do?" William asked from the floor. They looked down at him and realized his eyes were open.

"How long have you been listening?" Mike asked.

"I tuned in a minute or two ago. You couldn't bring me a cup of coffee, could you?"

Mike had the good grace to look sheepish. "Sorry, I'll be right back."

Nancy and William regarded each other for a moment in the quiet stillness of the morning. Then Nancy spoke softly to him. "I'm sorry."

"You have nothing to be sorry about. I was the one that acted like an idiot."

"You weren't an idiot. You were afraid."

"Yeah, I was an idiot. I could have gotten away from him after I'd woken up and discovered what I'd done. I could have run away. But I stayed with him because I was so desperate to feel some kind of affection after what happened with Michael."

They were quiet again and could hear Michael making a cup of coffee. "What would you like to do, then?" Nancy asked.

"I have no idea," William said. "Well, no that's not true. I need to get away from David. I think staying at Cordellia's would be a good idea, if she's willing to take me in."

"I'll call and find out. And if not, you can stay here." Nancy said.

Michael looked at Nancy with a surprised look on his face. It was nothing to the surprise he felt at actually saying the words out loud.

Chapter Thirty

Michael followed Nancy to the spare bedroom. It housed Nancy's office and showed the fruits of his labours. The walls were filled with graphic design contracts he had worked on along with pictures and photos that spoke to him. In the centre of the wall behind his computer hung a picture of his book cover. It was a gorgeous sight that never failed to take Michael's breath away.

Michael was moved every time he thought of what Nancy had accomplished in his life and hoped, one day, to make Nancy just as proud of him. However, right now they had more pressing matters to discuss.

"Are you sure that this is a good idea, having William stay with us?" Michael asked.

"Well, we're going to see if Cordellia can take him in first, sweetie. We're the backup."

"But it's William!"

"I know and until recently, you were married to him. He's my friend, too, or at least he was. No, he hasn't been himself or right for a while. Why shouldn't we help a friend?"

"Because it's William!"

Nancy came closer to him and took his hands in his. "Honey, I know this is hard for you, but would you turn your back on someone you used to love?"

"He hurt me."

"Fine, so turn the other cheek. You were with him for years. Can you just really look the other way at the exact moment he needs us? I love you Michael, but I thought your heart was bigger than that."

"But he hurt me. Do you think I can just get over that?"

"What did he do to you, really? Showed you his true colours."

"Part of me wants to see him suffer."

Nancy was aghast. "Are you telling me you get pleasure out of this?" He threw up his hands. "Mikey, part of what makes us better than the rest of the jerks out there in the world is that we can forgive and move on. We can let go and grow. There's no other way."

"I know that, I do. But hooking up with the man who hurt Blaine and me in the process? That's another kind of fucked up."

"Yes, I know that, I understand why you're upset. But we're bigger than all that because we got each other. You have to let go and move on. You can't keep living in the past. I wasn't in your past."

"Yes, you were."

"Not like I am now. Now we hold each other's hearts in our hands. Now it's different than it was before, for all of us; Blaine has Justin, Chuck has Sebastian, you have me. Even Poppy has Dava. We're all trying to find our happiness. Don't turn away from that."

"I'm trying not to."

"Let me put it this way. If you look away from the happiness and focus on the bad, you're turning your back on me." He gave Michael a pointed stare, straight into his gorgeous blue-grey eyes. "How do you think that makes me feel?"

Chapter Thirty-One

Poppy woke early.

She made a decaf coffee. The doctors had told her that regular coffee was bad for the baby. When the kid came out of her months from now, she planned to drink a vat of the stuff. She gazed down lovingly at her belly. "You'll be worth it, kid. I know you will."

She had thought a lot about whether she wanted a girl or a boy. Poppy had decided not to know the gender of the child. All she wanted was to love them as much as possible. She had told Blaine and Justin that last night.

"I just remember my parents. We were used as pawns between my parents, my sister and I. I'm never going to do that to my kid."

"Well, you didn't have gay parents. That's got to count for something, right?" said Justin.

Now, in the light of day, his words still brought a smile to her face. Poppy would give her kid the life she had never had. Sure, having a gay dad and a lesbian for a mother would make things interesting, but at least she knew who the father was. Justin had been the only man she had slept with in over a decade.

She was rubbing her little baby bump absentmindedly when the phone rang. Looking at the number, she saw it was Dava. She answered. "Hey, hot stuff."

"Hey yourself, beautiful. Did you get up to a lot of trouble last night?"

"No more than usual, why?"

"I called a few times but there was no answer."

"Sorry honey, I was hanging with the boys."

"Once a fag hag…"

"Always a fag hag. Wait, can lesbians even be fag hags? I thought that was only straight women."

"Search me. What are you up to today?"

"Nothing much. Want to pick me up, take me out for brunch, and then ravish me on the divan?"

"You own a divan?"

"No, but we could go find one. I know a good antiques place that would sell me one for cheap."

Dava's laughter was like music, full of light and magic. "You always know how to make me laugh, you know that?"

"Hey, it's one of my talents. So, what do you say?"

"I don't know about brunch. I have something to take care of today. Do you want to do dinner?"

Her voice sounded evasive and she sounded strained all of a sudden. "Dava, what's wrong?" Poppy hadn't meant to come right out and ask her, but her mouth and heart had other plans. "I know that there's been something up with you for a few weeks. You've been secretive and you're hiding something. I know you are. Can't you tell me?"

Dava was silent for a long time and, for a moment, Poppy wondered if she would even answer. Finally, she did. "Okay. Can you be ready in half an hour? I probably should have someone with me just in case something goes wrong."

That struck a note of fear in Poppy. "Dava, what's the matter?"

"I'll explain when I see you. It's okay, Poppy. Or it will be. Promise. Love you."

"Love you, too."

Dava hung up and Poppy was left holding the phone, wondering what this could possibly be about and feeling a knot of dread in her heart for the woman she loved.

Chapter Thirty-Two

Nancy was upset. The talk with Mike had left him a little shaken. He didn't like playing the heavy or enjoy giving Michael ultimatums, but that was the way it had to be done. The long and short of it was that William had been a friend before. There was no reason he couldn't be now.

Leaving Mike to his own devices, he went to check on William. He was sitting in the living room on the couch looking somewhat crestfallen. Nancy had remembered feeling like that, as if there weren't anyone in the world that would help him. He had turned to his Britney CDs back then. William had turned to drugs.

Sitting beside William, Nancy put on a brave face. "Look, William, I know things are rough right now, but at least you had the presence of mind to get away from a bad situation."

"But that's just it, Nance. I still want him. Does that sound fucking crazy?"

"How can you want someone who treats you that way? He beats you, Will."

"Even so, he told me he loved me. That has to amount to something, right?"

"What kind of love is that? You deserve a love that heals, not one that ruins you."

"You don't know what you're talking about."

"Yes, I do actually. So do you. Have you forgotten what happened with Blaine? What that bastard put him through?"

"I'd forgotten that," William admitted softly. "I'd forgotten they were even together."

"Come on, Will, it's been less than a year. You don't forget that easily."

"Yeah, but a month is like a year in the gay community. You know how fast things move here."

"But how could you forget what David did to Blaine? Or to Devon?"

"You can't expect me to believe that you care about what happened to Devon."

"I loved him." There was steel in Nancy's voice, and the look he gave William was cold.

William was quiet for a moment before he replied. "I'm sorry. I'm sorry, Nancy."

"It's okay."

"No, it's not. How did I get to this? How can I still want him? He treated me like crap this entire time, but I just keep hoping that somehow, I'll break through the wall, that underneath all the hurt and the nastiness, there's a man worth loving."

"You can't love someone if they won't love themselves, Will."

"So, how do I go about loving myself?"

"You never had a problem with that before."

"I've forgotten how. He's in my head, Nancy. I don't know how to get him out. Every time I look in the mirror, I hear his voice telling me that I'm not good enough, that I'm garbage, that I'm nothing. He called me 'broken,' Nancy."

Nancy was moved to put his arm around William and pull him close. "You're not broken William. You're not broken at all."

"But how do I stop feeling like this? I think he's the one who broke me."

Nancy held him close as William started to cry, tears sliding down his cheeks accompanied by sobs of the deepest sadness. He quieted down when there was a loud banging on

81

the front door.

They both looked at the door with growing apprehension. "Who do you think that is?" William asked.

"I don't know. We're not expecting anyone."

The banging increased. Then they heard a voice. It rang loud and clear, bellowing through the wood. "I know you're fucking in there! You fucking pussy! Come on out so I can teach you a lesson!"

It was David. He sounded crazed and maniacal, as if he had finally lost it. William shuddered, and Nancy pulled him into a hug, wrapping his arms around him as if to protect him from harm.

"Come the fuck out! You can't hide in there forever!"

"How did he know you were staying here?"

"I don't know. I often wondered if David had spies or something. He watches and sees everything," William whispered.

"No one is that omnipotent."

"Get the fuck out here!" David yelled. "What, are you fucking the she-male? Do you like how his cock tastes in your mouth?"

"He found Blaine," William said. "When he started working at the library." He talked over David's yelling as if he weren't there. Nancy wished that was the case. He wished they weren't hiding, afraid, in his own house. He was stronger than this. Enough. He stood.

"Where are you going?" William asked, clutching at his hand.

"I'm going to go take out the trash," Nancy said, his mouth set in a grim line.

"That won't be necessary. No one threatens me in my own house. I'll take care of him."

Nancy turned and saw Michael standing there, looking angry but somehow so very sexy. Nancy had never wanted him more.

"Don't go out there, Michael!" William cried. "You don't know what he's capable of!"

"Yes, I do. I know men like him and there's only one language they understand."

He strode to the door and ripped it open. Without saying a word, he landed a punch to David's face. "You think you can come here and threaten what's mine? You think you can do that and get away with it?"

He landed a punch to David's solar plexus causing David to bend over in pain. When he did, Michael slammed his elbow into David's back with all his weight. "You think you can come here and threaten the man I used to love? Just because I don't love him anymore doesn't mean I won't always care for him."

David had fallen to the ground and was trying to get up, struggling to his hands and knees. While he was in that position, Michael kicked him in the stomach, causing him to crumple into a heap. He kicked him one more time in the stomach and David let out a grunt.

"You're a piece of shit. You are nothing. You're the broken one, David, and you always will be."

David looked up at him from on the ground. "You're going to regret this. I'll make you pay."

"No, David, that's where you're wrong. I'm not afraid of you. You've hurt one of the people I love for the last time." Michael kicked David again in the ribs. "Now get the fuck out of here before I call the police."

Michael turned away from him, leaving David bleeding on the ground; he walked back inside, closed the door, and locked it.

Chapter Thirty-Three

Romilda was wondering if it was too early in the morning to have a Spanish coffee when the phone rang. She picked up the phone, wondering who would be on the other end. She hoped against hope it was Gaston but also dreaded it.

She took a deep breath and pressed the answer button on her phone. "Hello?"

"Romy, honey, it's Gaston. How are you?"

"I'm fine. I'm very fine, thank you."

"Do you still want to go for that drink?"

"It's eight o'clock in the morning."

"So, it's afternoon somewhere in the world, isn't it? Besides, I thought we'd go and see the sights, paint the town red."

"Red was never my colour, far too splashy."

"Always figured you for a pink kind of lady."

"Well, a pink lady is one of my favourite cocktails."

"Then let's go for one."

"Okay, when?"

"How about now?"

There was a knock on her door. On shaking legs, Romilda walked towards it and took another deep breath. She opened the door to find Gaston standing there holding his cell phone and he was smiling at her, his mouth in a wide grin.

"Hello, gorgeous."

"Hi. Hello." Romilda tried to keep the flutter out of her voice, but to no avail. Blushing, she opened the door wider. "Would you like to come in?"

"Nah, how about you come out? Let's go someplace, do something."

"Why?"

"Goodness, why not? I want to take you out on a date, that's why."

"I don't want to be a pity date, Gaston."

"Now, you wait just a darn minute."

Gaston came into her apartment and closed the door loudly behind him. "You listen to me. Are you listening?"

Romilda hadn't seen him this way before. He was all man and he was angry, but he didn't try to hit her, wasn't yelling at her and wasn't trying to make her agree to something against her will. "I'm listening."

"I think I love you. I don't care if you were a man or a Martian before—you're all woman now. You're beautiful and wonderful and I can't get you out of my head. You fill my waking hours with joy and my dreams with sex. I want you more than you could ever imagine. I don't care who you were, I only care about who you are now. I want you, not who you were. When you stop being afraid and start letting yourself live, then we can go somewhere and do something, maybe make something of ourselves together. You call me then, okay, Romy? You have my number."

He came close and kissed her softly, leaning into the kiss, giving her plenty of opportunity to pull away if she wanted to. She didn't want to budge. When his lips touched hers, she breathed a sigh of relief into him, and felt his answering sigh.

This is what she had been missing, what she had craved, what she had desired. When Gaston pulled away from the kiss, Romilda said, "Can I call you now?"

Chapter Thirty-Four

"I still don't see why you're being so secretive about this."

Poppy was trying to hold her patience and not get mad at Dava, but she was having a difficult time of it. They were in her car as Dava drove to a different part of the city, one that Poppy had never been to before. They had gone an hour outside of the city to a place at once foreign and desolate.

"I'll tell you when we get there."

"Dava, what is going on? You've been evasive for weeks now. Did you know that I was actually considering following you before you let me come along on this trip?"

Dava turned her head quickly, surprise in her eyes and then hurt. "That's low, Pops."

"I know it is, that was why I wouldn't have done it."

"Why would you have considered it, though?"

"Because you've been weird. You don't want to marry me, you've been missing for hours at a time, and you've gotten secretive lately. You won't talk to me or open up to me when I know something's wrong."

"Well, I'm opening up to you now. I'm taking you there, aren't I?"

"Where though, Dava? Where?"

"We're almost there now."

Poppy looked around her. The houses were old and falling down, a lot of them in desperate need of repair. Indeed, some didn't even look safe enough to live in, though a lot of people were doing just that. Poppy saw kids playing outside with their mothers, fathers drinking on the front stoop.

"What is this place?"

"You've never been here?" Dava asked. "I'm not surprised.

This is Lower Town. It used to be a pretty nice place when my folks lived here, but when the steel plant closed down, the whole place went to shit."

"Your folks?"

"Yes, my parents."

"You don't talk about your parents."

"I know. I'm sorry, Poppy. There are a lot of things I don't talk about, mostly because it's too difficult. I left all that behind me when I managed to leave here. Talking about all of that is like revisiting this place in my mind."

"What did you leave here, Dava?"

Dava stopped her car in front of a house, if you could call it that. It was the most run down of all the houses along the street, with yellowed grass and broken glass on the pavement. One of the windows was covered in cardboard and the screen door was hanging off the hinges.

Sitting on a lawn chair was one of the most disgusting men that Poppy had ever seen. Even just looking at him made her wonder when he had last had a shower. He was well over six feet tall with a large beer gut. There were cans littering the ground around him like prehistoric diamonds.

He saw the car stop and looked into the window. Seeing them, he heaved himself up off the chair and started towards the car. The man looked angry and Poppy was shocked to see a look of fear on Dava's face.

"Who is that man, Dava?"

Shaking, Dava took a deep breath. "He's my husband, Poppy. I'm married."

Chapter Thirty-Five

"What do you mean your fucking husband?"

Poppy was sure that her head was swimming and she hadn't heard correctly. There was no way she had heard properly. She looked at Dava, waiting for an explanation. Dava could only sit there as tears ran down her face.

"Why have you never told me about this before? We've known each other for a while now. I told you all about Colleen. How could you keep this from me?"

"Don't," Dava said. "Don't accuse me of keeping anything from you. I'm showing you now, aren't I?" She clutched Poppy's hand. "Don't judge me before you know the whole story."

"And what is the whole story, Dava? What's going on here?"

They were interrupted by a thundering bang on the window. "That you, Dava, you fucking cunt?" the man bellowed. "You come back at last? I told you that you would amount to nothing. Get out of the fucking car."

He began banging on the window again, then raised his beer bottle and smashed it on the car, shattering it into shards of brown glass. "Get out, you fucking cunt bitch. You think you can leave me with nothing? What about our boys, huh?"

"Drive Dava, just drive away right now."

"No, I came here to end this."

"You can file another way, I'm not having you put yourself into danger to prove a point."

"You think this is about proving a point to you? What about proving to myself what I'm worth? That I'm worth more than that?"

When the man went to take another swing at the car window and then grabbed the handle, Poppy screamed, "Drive, Dava, drive!"

Putting the car into gear, Dava sped away from the house and back through the rundown part of the city. The entire time, she spoke.

"When we got married, it was nice. I knew I was a lesbian, but you couldn't be one in those days. I loved Randy as much as I could, as much as any woman could I guess, given the state of him. Then the drinking started."

She wiped at her eyes with her fingers and continued. "It got worse. I got pregnant with one boy and then with another and spent most of my life in that house making sure they were safe. When they were old enough, I got away. I just packed some of my stuff, took out all the money from the account and left. I haven't been back since. That was ten years ago."

"What happened to your kids, Dava?"

"Well, I saw Josh last week and Alex is on vacation with his wife."

Poppy looked at her incredulously. "How old are your kids?"

"They're in their thirties. They have good lives and are nothing like their father." She stifled a sob. "I suppose you think I'm weak."

"How could I ever think that?"

"Living in a house like that for so long, letting myself get beaten. Not standing up to him until it was almost too late and bringing up my kids in that kind of a home."

"I think you're the bravest woman I know," Poppy said softly. "Come on, let's go get a cup of tea."

"I wouldn't say no to something stronger."

Poppy let out a watery laugh and kissed Dava on the cheek. "You got it, babe."

Chapter Thirty-Six

Cordellia tried to look her best. It had been a long time since she had a man to dazzle. Not that she had to impress anyone, least of all a man, but it certainly helped.

When Joe knocked on the door, she took a deep breath, fluffed her hair in the mirror and then quickly smoothed it back down. She had never cared this much about what she looked like when she had been with him before.

Opening the door, she smiled when she saw him, his hair dark grey, peppered with white. He had the deepest brown eyes that she could just fall into. It was a few seconds before she realized that she was staring.

"Sorry."

"Nothing to be sorry about, Cordy. Nothing to be sorry about at all. You look ravishing."

"I was thinking the same thing about you."

He had worn a pair of dark blue jeans and had paired them with a white shirt and a dark corduroy blazer. She had treated herself to a new dress and it flowed around her ankles as if made from gossamer silk. It was in a beautiful light blue, one of her favourite colours.

Joe seemed to read her mind. "You always looked stunning in that colour. Isn't the front cut a bit low, though?" He grinned at her.

She slapped his arm. "Hey now, a woman has to show off what she's got, even if they do hang down to my ankles."

"Never. They're still as beautiful as they were when we were younger."

"Flirt. You need new glasses." She grabbed her purse from the hallway table. "Where are we going? "

"It's a surprise."

"You know I don't like surprises."

"I also know that you love surprises, but always pretend not to like them. Live large, Cordy! Be brave!"

"Oh, believe me, I am. My heart is hammering in my chest."

"Why do you have to be nervous around me?"

"Oh, we can save that for another time."

"Okay then, but we'll revisit this conversation. Now your chariot awaits."

She leaned forward and kissed him softly on the lips. "Silly man."

"Yes, but I'm your man. You ready?"

"For you? Always."

She closed the door then turned around and stopped when she saw what was awaiting her on the street in front of her house. "Joe? Why is a limousine sitting there?"

"That's our ride."

"Our ride? Where do you plan on taking me in a limousine?"

"You'll have to find out, won't you? Now stop asking questions and just get in."

With her heart thrumming with excitement, Cordellia did just that.

Chapter Thirty-Seven

Rebecca's phone rang from within the depths of her purse. She could hear the opening bars to "Don't Want No Short Dick Man" playing. It seemed appropriate. What woman did? Plus, it served two purposes: it let guys know what she was looking for and kept them away at the same time.

She looked at the number on the screen and saw the name I'm an Asshole. It was Dylan. She took a breath before answering in her deepest, sexiest voice. "Hello."

"Rebecca? It's Dylan. How are you?"

"I'm feeling rather hungry. I have an itch I need scratched."

"You feeling okay?"

She switched back to her normal voice. "Seriously? I do my best phone sex voice and that's all I get? Am I feeling okay? Please."

"I'm sorry. Do you want me to try again?"

"Nah, moment's gone. What can I do for you?"

"Well, I was wondering if I could see you again."

"I don't know. You were a complete douchebag to my best friend. That doesn't really put you in my good books, if you know what I mean."

"Look, the relationship between me and Devon is complicated."

"So, his dick is bigger than yours. I get it."

"Oh no, it isn't."

"What, you've compared your dick to your brother's? What kind of a family did you grow up in?"

"That's not what I meant."

"Sure, sounded like it."

Dylan took a deep breath and let out a laugh. "Are you always like this?"

"Like what?"

"So frustrating, yet, so captivating?"

Her heart skipped a beat despite herself. "Captivating huh? That's the best you can do?"

"How about this? I can't get the sight of you out of my mind. The sound of your voice turns me on, and I had a dream about you last night."

"Was I naked? If so, I'm sorry for that. You can wash your eyes out with bleach if you need to."

"Would you stop joking around for a moment? I'm trying to pay you a compliment and you're taking a dig at yourself. Don't do that. Self-deprecating humour is only funny in certain situations. This wasn't one of them."

"Oh. Okay." She really didn't know what to say to that. No man had ever said such nice things about her, let alone dreamt of her. That had to be a first. "So, what did you call for?"

"I wanted to see you again to find out if the real you compares to the dream you."

She took a breath. He was asking her out on a date! Wait a minute. "You want to go out on a date? Like an actual date?"

"Yes, that's what people generally do when they're trying to get to know each other."

"Okay. Um, when?"

"How about now?"

There was a knock on her door. "That better not be you."

"And what if it is?"

Chapter Thirty-Eight

Opening her door, Rebecca saw Dylan standing there with large grin. She wanted to be mad at him for just showing up, but that grin was so fucking sexy and his green eyes sparkled like two emeralds.

Still, she had a reputation to uphold. "What the fuck are you doing here?"

"A guy can't come by and say hello?"

"Not when said guy doesn't know my address."

"I called Devon and asked him. He told me."

"That little bitch. Why would he give you my personal information?"

"Maybe he thinks we'll be good for each other?"

"Hell, I'm surprised you're talking to each other. You weren't very nice to him at the bar the other night."

"I have my reasons. Why don't you come out with me, and I'll tell you all about them?"

"What makes you think I want to?"

"There was a spark between us, right? Or, am I just imagining that?"

"Oh, you sure know how to talk to a lady. I must have responded to your animal magnetism or something."

"Look, I called my brother to be able to talk to you. That has to count for something."

"Okay, how about this? You go out three times in the next three weeks and do brother stuff. How's that for a trade?"

"You're only willing to go out with me if I patch things up with Devon?"

"Yep."

"Why is it so important to you?"

"Because it's important to him."

"Bullshit."

"No, it's not. You haven't heard him talk about you, how much he misses you. How you rarely talk. It would mean a lot to him, Dylan."

He sighed. "He really means that much to you, huh?"

She smiled at him. "He's my family. I would do anything for him."

"I've never heard anyone say that about Devon. Okay, you have a deal."

"Excellent." She grabbed her purse. "Let's go then. We can take my car."

"Where are we going? Did you want to grab a drink?"

"Nope, you're going to take me shopping."

The look on Dylan's face was priceless. "Shopping? Really?"

"Yes, really." She looked down at his sneakers. "Good, you wore sensible shoes." She smiled. "You're going to need them."

"Why? We're just going shopping."

She gave him a wide grin. "Babe, most women shop. I have turned it into an art form and an Olympic sport. I don't just shop, I'm always in training. Do you know how badass you have to be to get a pair of Jimmy Choo shoes on a Black Friday sale? Seriously, you want tough, go to one of those and survive."

She closed her door and locked it. "Prepare to be amazed."

Chapter Thirty-Nine

Devon was contemplating what to do with the day. He had gotten up late and had no plans. He had called Rebecca to see if she wanted to do something, but the call went straight to voice mail.

He didn't do well with being alone; it was something he was trying to learn, to be comfortable with himself. But he had always been surrounded by people, wanted by others, desired by some. You feed off that, he realized. It had been a long time since he had been comfortable in his own skin.

Thinking about it more, perhaps it wasn't him who was desired rather than a quick end to a need, the explosion rather than the buildup. He had been a hooker for so long, he didn't know how to do anything else. He'd saved so much money from bartending and hooking, he didn't have to do anything else for a while. This should have filled him with glee, but instead it left him listless and with a lot of time to fill.

Standing on his balcony, he watched the cars down below, everyone going somewhere with a destination in mind. He was drifting through life. He had to find something to do, the only problem was that he had no idea what that would be. Sighing to himself, he went back inside for another cup of coffee when his phone rang.

He saw it was Curtis. His heart leapt a little. The coffee the other night had gone well, and Curtis had walked him home. He had promised to call. And now he did. A man who kept his promises? This was new.

Should I answer? he thought. Do I let Curtis know the real me?

He'd start by taking the call. "Hey."

"Hey yourself, handsome. What are you up to today?"

"A fuckload of nothing."

"Don't have anything planned?"

"Nope, not a thing. I'm a little bored actually."

"Good. Come out on your balcony."

"Why?"

"Just do it."

"Okay."

Devon went out on the balcony again. The sun felt good on his skin. He realized he probably should have put on pants and a shirt, but he didn't care. "Okay, I'm on the balcony. Now what?"

"Look down, handsome."

Devon did so and saw Curtis standing there holding his phone in one hand and bag of takeout food in the other. "Why didn't you just ring up to my apartment?"

"I don't know. This seemed more romantic. You hungry?"

"Yeah, for you."

"What?"

Shit. He had said that out loud. Shit fuck shit. "I'm always hungry."

"So, you going to invite me up?"

"Sure." His heat beat a little faster. "Just ring up and I'll buzz you in."

"Cool! See you in a moment."

Curtis disappeared from the sidewalk and a moment later his phone rang. He buzzed Curtis in, then stood there, wondering what the hell was going on. He hadn't slept with Curtis yet, why was Curtis interested in him?

Well, he would rectify that right now. Stripping off his boxer shorts, he waited for the knock on the door. When it came, he went to it and opened it. Curtis was there with a smile, which widened when he took all of Devon in.

"Nice. Very nice. Why don't you put some clothes on, though? Eating breakfast sandwiches from Talia's can get a little messy."

"Don't you want to sleep with me? Don't you want to fuck?"

"Oh, I do." Curtis motioned to his groin and Devon could see a large bulge in Curtis's jeans. "You turn me on, there's no doubt about that, but I just want to get to know you a little before we hit the sack. How's that sound?"

Devon stared at him. He was in shock. No one had ever turned down an opportunity to sleep with him. He was standing there naked in front of Curtis and yet Curtis had not become a puddle of need. "I'm sorry, I'm sorry. God, I'm such an idiot."

He went to his bedroom and began pulling on a t-shirt, another pair of boxers and a pair of jeans. "I don't know what I was thinking."

"You were thinking with your dick. That's all fine and dandy, but I like the guy I met the other night who was thinking with his mind. That turns me on more."

"I'm sorry."

"Don't be sorry. Do I turn you on?"

"Obviously, otherwise, I wouldn't have answered the door naked and hard for you."

"Good, then we'll have a lot to look forward to when the moment arrives. In the meantime, let's eat. Looking at a sexy naked man makes me ravenous."

Chapter Forty

"So, you still haven't told me how shopping is a sport. Don't you just go in, get what you want, and go out?"

They were heading towards the mall. The city had three of them and they were driving to the largest of the three. It had more stores than Rebecca actually shopped in and all the brands she liked. Now, she knew that it didn't have to be a brand name to mean quality, but it didn't hurt.

Rebecca looked at Dylan in the passenger seat. "You really haven't shopped with a woman before, have you?"

"No. Go in, get it, get out. That's how I shop."

"That's how all men shop. It's disgusting and completely boring. I don't just shop, I dance across the isles. I don't merely buy items, I answer their call."

"Still though, you buy stuff and take it home. That's shopping."

"You're a man, so you can't possibly understand."

"Yeah, I guess my high level of testosterone keeps me so grounded, I can't dance."

She didn't expect this reply and burst out laughing. "I've never heard it put quite that way, but you just described most men who try to shop. Women view it as a religious experience, men just grab what they want and leave." She changed tracks. "So, why do you and Devon not get along?"

"It's a long story."

"I like stories. Try me."

Dylan was quiet for a moment as if he were trying to find the right words. When he spoke again it was without the bravado he'd been wearing since he had showed up this morning. Instead, it was the true him shining through. "It's what he did."

"What did he do?"

"It broke my family apart."

"Jesus, Dylan, am I going to have to pull every word out of your mouth with my fingers?"

He gave her a wicked grin and wiggled his eyebrows. "Now that sounds promising."

"Stop stalling and tell me."

He was quiet again but seemed to be concentrating, as if he were trying to assemble the words mentally before he spoke them out loud.

"Devon was always bumming money from my parents. He was always short, always needing a loan of some sort. My mother never said no to him. She said no to my sister and me plenty of times. Then the loans got bigger. She bought him a house, paid for a car. We found out later that she was using her pension to give him money and buy him things and was going without food to do so."

Rebecca was quiet while he went on and didn't know if she could speak until he was done. She wanted to say something comforting to ease the pain he wore on his face, but there was nothing she could say.

"My mother died penniless. She had nothing left to leave us. It all went to Devon. He's tried to mend the burned bridges between all of us, but it's tough to love him."

"But do you?"

"Yes, he's my brother."

"You can start there, then. You can start there."

She reached out with her free hand and gave his thigh a squeeze. "Thank you for telling me."

"You're welcome. You're easy to talk to."

Rebecca parked the car. "I only hope I'm just as easy to shop with. Come on sailor, grab your comfortable shoes and let's go! Time's a wasting!"

Chapter Forty-One

Blaine had to admit it. He was nervous.

Granted, he didn't have a lot of experience in meeting in-laws. Hell, he'd never been in a position to do so. David's parents were dead and the other relationships he'd been in hadn't progressed to the meeting-the-parents stage.

He wasn't worried. If Justin's parents were anything like him, they would get along like a house on fire. For some strange reason, however, Justin looked more nervous than he was. He took in his strained face and the white knuckles on the steering wheel as he drove. There was even some sweat on his forehead. Justin even looked a little pale.

"What's wrong, handsome man?"

"What? Nothing. Nothing's wrong."

"I know when something's bothering you."

"Nothing's bothering me. Hey, what do you say we blow off my parents and go have a burger somewhere? Get drunk and fuck like rabbits."

Letting out a laugh, Blaine squeezed Justin's leg. "What? I've been looking forward to this for a long time! I want to see where you came from, who made you! They'll be part of my family now."

"I wouldn't be too sure of that."

"Why do you sound so serious? What gives?"

"There's a reason I haven't introduced you to them. I hardly ever see them, really, but they saw me walking with you in front of the GLBTQ Library and my father called me to find out who you were."

"What did you tell them?"

"That you were my lover and my partner."

Justin's voice had gone hard and grim. He was staring straight ahead, and Blaine could see the rough set of his mouth as it grimaced.

"Well, don't say that like it's a bad thing."

"It's not, Blaine, it's the best thing in the world. You're the most wonderful thing that's happened to me."

"Then what's the problem?"

"You'll see soon enough."

"You can't just drop a bomb on me like that and expect to not give me any details. What gives, babe? What's going on?"

Justin took a moment to respond. They were turning into the Golden Circle, a high-priced area of the city that catered to the rich and wealthy. "My parents have never approved of me."

"How can they not? I mean, you're a fucking lawyer for crying out loud! You've helped many when they didn't have a voice. How could they not approve of you?"

"It's not my job they don't approve of. It's my choice of lifestyle."

They were pulling into a driveway. Justin stopped the car and turned off the engine. Blaine took off his seat belt and turned to Justin. "What? They don't like the fact that you're gay?"

Justin didn't reply; however, he had turned even paler. Following his gaze, Blaine saw a man and a woman standing on the front stoop, regarding the car with what could only be described as cold disdain.

Chapter Forty-Two

Justin's mother came down the stairs.

Blaine watched her move in graceful, elegant strides towards them as they got out of the car, and he tried to take them in. Justin's mother wore a long, floor-length dress in a black and white floral print, gloves, and pearls around her neck. Her hair was styled in an impossible up-do. His father, on the other hand, stood at the front door with his arms crossed, dressed in a black suit with a grey tie. Blaine felt quite under dressed in a pair of jeans and a comfortable t-shirt.

Justin's mother held out her arms and uttered in a deep, dramatic voice: "My son! Come and give mother a hug!"

Blaine was struck dumb and unable to look away as Justin's mother approached her boy and wrapped Justin in a tight hug. She stepped back and regarded Justin as if she had bestowed upon him a blessing of some sort.

Clearing his throat, Justin motioned to Blaine. "This is my partner, Mom. This is Blaine. Blaine, this is my mother, Victoria."

Victoria gave Blaine an up and down look that took in everything about him in an instant. Blaine felt as if he were being x-rayed. She did the same look one more time and then spoke. "So, you're the cock my son is sucking on? He did always love his pacifier when he was a child, you know. I always tell new parents not to use them as the child might grow up with a fondness for dick later in life."

Blaine nearly choked on words unuttered. He tried to arrange his face into one of openness instead of shock and approached her with his hand out. "Hello Victoria, I'm Blaine."

"Yes, I heard your name. And I'm not Victoria to you, I am Mrs. Chase."

"Mom," Justin said, exasperated.

"Don't you Mom me, he should know to respect his elders."

"I'm sorry, Mrs. Chase. Won't happen again."

"Too right, it won't." She gave Blaine another cold look and turned towards the front door. "Well, you're here now. Might as well come in."

"Thanks, Mom, so kind of you."

Victoria Chase turned and almost spat on her son. "You could use a lesson in respecting your elders, too. I suppose you got the lip from him?" She jerked a thumb at Blaine.

"Your son is one of the kindest men I know. I'm sure he didn't mean anything by it."

"Yes, and I'm sure you know a lot of men." She motioned again. "Come inside then."

Justin's father was still standing in front of the door. Justin held out his hand to his father, but his father didn't take it. So Justin let it fall and simply said, "Hey Dad. This is Blaine. Blaine, this is my father, Gregory."

"Nice to meet you, Mr. Chase."

Gregory Chase ignored Blaine completely and instead spoke to Justin. "So. Still a fag then?"

"I can't change who I am, Dad."

"Funny, I thought that your kind of people changed whenever they wanted to."

"Now let's not fight," Victoria said. "At least until we're inside. After all, what would the neighbours say?"

Chapter Forty-Three

The inside of the house was immaculate. Blaine took off his shoes, hesitant to step into the house lest he bring in dirt. The foyer was even more impressive than the outside of the house. All Blaine could see was a sea of marble and black wood. It reminded him more of a bank than a home.

Victoria and Gregory had already walked into the living room, leaving Blaine and Justin alone. Blaine gave Justin a panicked look, "Why didn't you tell me?"

"What, that my parents are fag-hating WASPs? What could I have said, 'Oh, by the way honey, my parents hate who I am?' Would that have worked for you?"

"Well, some warning would have been nice. I mean, you know my parents."

"They are my parents, too."

"Then who are these jokers?"

"They're the people who gave me life. But I have to love them."

"Why?"

"Because without them, I wouldn't be alive to meet you."

Blaine tensed at first when Justin leaned in and kissed him softly on the lips, but hearing nothing from the rest of the house, Blaine kissed him back. "When you put it that way, it sounds like I owe your parents a thank you as well. I'll just keep it to myself, though."

"Probably a good idea, babe."

From the living room, Victoria's voice rang out, "Are you two coming, or not?"

"Darling," Gregory said. "Don't say words like 'coming' around them. You don't know what it's apt to do to them."

Victoria let out a loud peal of laughter and was still laughing when Blaine and Justin went into the living room. The laughter stopped immediately. "We'd invite you for dinner, but we don't want you here. Would you like a drink?"

"That's very kind of you," Blaine said softly, trying to keep the situation calm. He could tell that Justin was getting angry, he could see it in his stance.

"Oh, kindness has nothing to do with it. We know you all like your booze, we just want to make sure you're not dehydrated on the ride home."

"That does it!" Justin yelled.

"Of course, darling, we're only giving you a shot or a half glass. Don't want you both getting messy in here."

"I've fucking had it with the two of you," he spat out.

"Watch your language," Gregory said.

"I fucking will not. All I've done is love you. You are my parents and they say that a son is supposed to love his parents. When I came out to you at eighteen, you shunned me, wouldn't talk to me but then tried to convince me that something was wrong with me when all I wanted was to be happy."

"Well, darling we do want you to be happy, not die of AIDS like the rest of your people," Victoria said.

"Well, speaking as the spokesperson for my people, you two can go fuck yourselves with an iron poker." He pulled Blaine towards him and wrapped an arm around Blaine's waist. "I love this man with all my heart and every fibre of my being. I'm going to marry him, and I don't want either of you to be there."

Putting a hand to her chest, Victoria gave Justin a hurt look. "Darling, if you love him with all your heart, that doesn't leave anything to love us!" She gestured at Gregory and herself.

"Exactly."

With that, Justin took hold of Blaine's hand and they walked out of the house where Justin slammed the front door as hard as he could.

Chapter Forty-Four

They drove home.

Justin was quiet, gripping the steering wheel with white-knuckled fingers. Blaine tried to find the words he wanted to say, but they were lost amidst a sea of emotions. Finally, he just said, "What just happened back there?"

"You got to meet my parents for the first and last time."

"Did we really need to go through all of that? Why didn't you warn me?"

"Warn you that, what, my parents hated me?" Justin let out a rough breath. "Yeah, that's something that you can prepare your loved one for. Sure thing."

"Justin, I get why you're upset. If my mother talked to me like that, I'd be pissed off too."

"You don't get it."

"Then try to make me understand."

They pulled up in front of their building. "I've been out as gay since I was eighteen. Do you have any idea what it's like to do everything you can to get your parents to love you and they continue to set you up with girls, hoping for a miracle? Hoping that this one will make their son not gay."

Blaine took Justin's hands in his own. "You know that I have no idea what that's like. I couldn't even begin to understand what you're feeling right now. For years, I thought I didn't have a mother or father and now that I do, I don't know what to do with myself. I couldn't imagine what you went through growing up. It must have been horrible for you."

"It was. I had a few boyfriends and a few fag hag friends. But there's something missing when you don't have your parents love, you know? Something just felt wrong with my life. I can't count the number of times I hoped and wished and prayed for them to look at me with something approaching love. Maybe they did when I was a kid, but not when I came out of the closet."

"Why didn't they kick you out if they were so unhappy with it?"

"What, and let the neighbours talk? It was bad enough that I left home at eighteen after I came out. I couldn't stand another moment under their roof."

"So, you have nothing to do with them?"

"We do Christmas and holidays. That's it. I'm an only child and my parents always hoped for grandchildren. My mother kept passing me pictures of kids from orphanages, hoping that one of them would strike my fancy."

Blaine said nothing for a little bit, just listened to the sound of Justin's breathing. It was slowing as he got himself under control. When it was softer and Justin looked calmer, Blaine spoke again.

"So, why did you introduce them to me?"

Justin was quiet for a moment and Blaine listened to him breathing. There were times, like this one, where he swore he could hear the beat of Justin's heart. When Justin spoke, his voice was soft, his face calm.

"I wanted them to meet the man that I will be spending the rest of my life with. I wanted them to know that, after everything, I had found love at last."

A tear escaped Justin's left eye and sneaked down his cheek, leaving a trail that shone like glass on his skin. It stopped at his lips. Blaine leaned forward and kissed Justin, hoping that he could take the sadness away from him.

Chapter Forty-Five

Talia's was a family-run restaurant. They had all kinds of food and all of it was homemade. To Devon, the restaurant always smelled of cinnamon and cloves. Talia herself came out to take their order.

"Curtis! Honey, long time no see! Why haven't you come to see me lately?"

"I can't eat here all the time."

"Yes, you can! You're family, I've told you that before!"

"Well, yes, but I would have no money left if all I did was eat here."

"Who needs money when you have family?" She gave him a roguish wink. Smiling, she turned to look at Devon for the first time and the smile slowly faded away. "Curtis, sweetie, what are you doing with this piece of trash?"

"Hey now, he's my date."

"Oh honey, you can do better. You don't want the town bike for a boyfriend, do you?"

"Talia, please. I think Devon is sweet."

"Well, I have my own ideas of what he might taste like." She turned to Devon. "You hurt my boy Curtis and I'll break both your arms and both your legs, got it?"

Devon nodded. "Got it."

"Good." The smile returned, and she gave Curtis a pat on the cheek. "Right this way."

She brought them to a table with a window view. "Now you guys can check out eye candy while you talk. Lord knows there's enough of it in this town." She left menus on the table and walked over to greet another customer.

They were quiet for a moment. A waitress came and filled

their coffee cups.

"I'll be back in a minute to take your orders," she said and left with a smile.

Devon was now more nervous than ever. "Curtis, I—I don't know what to say."

"About her instant dislike for you, or the comment about being the town bike?"

"Both actually. Women love me usually, but she's seen me here before."

"So, what did she mean?" Curtis's voice was soft. Not angry or demanding. Just quiet as if he asked out of curiosity rather than some sense of urgency.

Trying to assemble the words before he spoke them didn't seem to be the way to go. Instead, he just spoke from the heart. "Look, I wasn't a very nice guy before. I had a chance at love, at true love, and I blew it because I was blowing other guys."

Curtis nodded and grinned at him, motioning for him to continue.

"I guess I was a male prostitute. I prefer the term 'call guy.' Sounds much classier. If you had the money, I would do you or let you do me. Anything for a dollar. None of them meant anything to me, except for Nancy. I loved him with almost all my heart, but there was a piece of it I kept for myself. That piece let me still go out hooking."

"That must have been very lonely for you."

Devon was shocked at Curtis's words. He had never thought about it that way. "Yeah, it was until Nancy came along."

"So, what happened?"

"I accepted money for services from a very bad guy, someone who was personally connected to Nancy and all of his friends. An abuser. I figured that at three-hundred bucks for an hour's work, I didn't care if he was Satan himself." He took a swallow of coffee. "I should have."

He almost wavered then, not sure if he could continue but at that moment, Curtis reached out and took a hold of his hand. It was such a simple gesture, and it meant the world to Devon.

"It's okay, go on," Curtis said.

"He hurt me. Badly. I went to him when I could have gone to Nancy. Even after he had beat me enough to make me incapacitated for weeks, I still gave the guy a blowjob." The enormity of how he had fucked up and taken Nancy for granted hit him again and, despite himself, a few tears leaked out of his eyes. He wiped them away quickly.

"I spent a whole month mourning Nancy and what we had together. Afterwards, I swore to change my life and not let love slip by a second time." He sighed. "You must think I'm a total sleaze."

"Oh, I already knew."

"What?" Devon was thunderstruck.

"That you were a male call boy? Of course, I knew!"

"How did you know?"

"I've seen you around, handsome. And you really got around. A community this small? You know that everyone else knows your business."

"Oh." Devon suddenly felt very small and vulnerable.

However, Curtis reached across the table and took Devon's right hand to his lips. He kissed the palm, letting his lips linger there. When he looked up at Devon again, he was smiling. "Thank you for telling me and being honest, though. Now, did you want to get the pancakes? They're freaking awesome."

Chapter Forty-Six

Cordellia didn't know what to think.

She had never ridden in a limousine before. It was so decadent, and the leather seats were soft like butter. She sat in the back with Joe, nestled up against him. He had his arm around her, and she could smell his cologne. It was the one he always wore and, to her, it smelled of leather and spice.

Joe hummed a soft tune as he held her, and she was almost lulled to sleep. Outside it was still daylight but only just. Dusk was setting in, and it had turned the sky a soft shade of violet. Cordellia thought nothing had ever been more beautiful; the scent of Joe, the purple sky, and the music of his heart beat. She nestled in closer.

"You comfortable?"

"Yes, I am. I feel delicious."

"I'm sure you taste delicious too, but we'll have to save that for later."

Letting out a laugh, she sat up and looked at him. "Joe, not that I don't appreciate it, but what is all this about?"

For a moment, she wondered whether he would answer her. All he said in reply was: "I want to do something that I should have done years ago. I want to do it right."

"You've done everything right, Joe. Everything. I was the one who ran, choosing to be alone rather than with you. You've done nothing wrong."

"I know that, but you always said we should try to live without regret as much as we can. I only have one regret, and I mean to fix that tonight."

"Joe." She put a hand on his chest and felt his heart beating under her fingers. "I don't need anything fancy. I just want you. Now that I have you, I don't ever want to let go."

"That's good to hear. You know I love you, Cordellia, more than anything."

The driver knocked on the window and lowered it slightly. "We're here, sir."

"Excellent."

The driver got out and opened the back door of the limo. Joe got out first and then held out his hand to her. She smiled, feeling like a schoolgirl on her first date. She was still smiling when she stepped out of the car and saw what was waiting for them.

It was a private dinner for two. There was a small bistro table with a red and white checked table cloth. There was a bottle of wine on the table with two glasses and a basket of food sitting on the grass beside it.

The table was overlooking the city. She could see the lights of the city and they twinkled brighter as more came on. The whole of it looked alive, almost as if it were lit up just for them. Cordellia turned to look at Joe and could see some of the lights reflected in his eyes.

"Joe, what is all this?"

"What, a man can't take his girl out for a romantic dinner?"

"Well, you could have just taken me to a restaurant. Again, what is all this?"

"This is romance, honey. Let a guy be romantic, huh? I've had precious little occasion for that in a long time."

Her heart fluttered in her chest. "Okay."

"Will you be eating now, sir?"

"Yes, Geoffrey."

"Excellent. Shall I serve the food now?"

"That would be most appreciated." Joe held out his hand to her. "Come, my lady. Dinner awaits."

Chapter Forty-Seven

She had had far too much wine.

The driver had produced plates of Lobster Niçoise salad. Joe had remembered that it was her favourite. There was even white and red wine. They had made their way through the white and were now on the red. When she had finished every bite of her salad, the driver had produced two chocolate tortes, one for each of them.

They giggled like youngsters, feeding each other forkfuls until it, too, was gone. When all the dinner dishes were cleared away, Geoffrey produced a small violin. He began to play a soft melody that perfectly complimented the feeling of the night that had come upon them while they were eating. It was somehow wistful and wishful at the same time.

Geoffrey had even lit candles and put them on the table. Joe looked so beautiful by candlelight. Then again, everyone did. She sat back, a little bit of wine left in her glass, and looked at Joe. "I can't tell you how lovely this has been. I've never been so spoiled!"

"Well, you can't say that romance is dead, can you?"

Letting out a laugh, Cordellia gave him a wink and clinked her glass to his. "Not with you, it's not."

"I'm glad to hear that, Cordy. You make my heart happy and my soul sing."

"Oh, you old charmer, you."

"I mean it Cordellia." He was serious all of a sudden. He put down his wine glass and took hers and put it aside. He took her hands in his. "When you showed up at my place the other day, I thought that my prayers had been answered. Do you know how many nights, days, hours I wished for you?"

"Can't have been more than I wished for you."

"I think I got you beat on this one. Even when you were with me, I knew that you would leave. I hoped and prayed that you would choose to stay with me, but you didn't. Every hour of every day since, I wished for you."

"How could you know that I would leave?"

"I could see it in your eyes. You looked like a deer in the headlights. It was like you were afraid of yourself, afraid of what you wanted. Afraid to admit it to yourself."

They were quiet for a moment. Cordellia had tears in her eyes. She reached across the table and took Joe's hand. "I'm not afraid now."

"I know you're not. I've never been afraid of what we had. That's why I planned this evening. I wanted to celebrate something."

"What?"

"This," Joe said, producing a ring box from his pocket. "I would be remiss if I didn't tell you how much I love you. How much I don't want to let you go now that I have your heart in my hand, and you have mine. I want to spend the rest of our lives together, however long that may be. Will you do me the honour of becoming my wife?"

Cordellia didn't even need to think about it, but she asked anyway, "Are you sure?"

Joe let out a breath. "Babe, I've never been surer of anything in my whole entire life."

"Neither have I." Cordellia felt euphoric, as if everything in her life had led to this beautiful, perfect moment. "I would be honoured to be your wife. The answer is yes."

Joe opened the box and Cordellia saw an impossibly beautiful ring. It looked like a star encased in black velvet. Joe pulled the ring out of the box and slid it slowly onto her finger. Where its brilliance shone upon her hand.

Chapter Fifty-Eight

When they had gone out front to see if David was still there, a bloody mess on the driveway asphalt was all that remained. He was gone.

"I still can't believe you punched him for me," William said, wearing a huge smile.

"I didn't do it only for you. I also did it for Blaine and because David dared to come to the home I share with Nancy. I did it because he deserved it. Lord knows it's about high time that someone gave him a dose of his own medicine."

Nancy looked at him with a roguish grin. "I never knew you were such a tough man."

"I'm plenty strong, thank you very much."

"What happens if he comes back?" William asked. "I don't know what to do. He knows where I live. I don't have anyone to turn to."

"Hey, now. You have us and I'm sure the other guys will come around eventually. You can't lose hope. At least you got away."

"Yeah, but I'm still alone," William said, looking at Nancy.

Nancy sighed, "Always the drama queen. I'm going to call Cordellia. She'll talk some sense into you, she always does for me when I need help. She may even give you a place to stay."

"She wouldn't do that."

"How do you know unless you ask her? Plus, she gave David a talking to once that left him looking like he had been whipped. I'll call her tomorrow. In the meantime, we're going to go out and get drunk."

Michael gave him a quizzical look. "Do you really think that's such a good idea after what we've been through tonight?"

"Oh honey, I don't know about you, but I could use a drink. Hold up, I have an idea."

He took out his phone and dialed Chuck. He picked up on the first ring.

"Yeah?"

"Hey Chucky Cheese, it's Nancy."

"Hey Britney, what's up?"

"I'm calling an emergency meeting at The Cabin. Mike and William are with me. Can you call Justin and Blaine? And bring Sebastian? I'll call Poppy and see if she can come with Dava."

"You're bringing William? What gives? I thought we were supposed to hate his guts forever and ever."

"It's a long story. I'll need a drink to tell it."

"Cosmos all around?"

"Make mine a Mai Tai and we're set."

"Oooh, a Mai Tai. Must be a good story if you're getting big-boy drinks."

"Hey, a cosmo is a big boy drink."

Chuck laughed. "Anything you have to sip daintily is so not a big boy drink."

"Says the man that chugs beer like a straight guy."

Chapter Fifty-Nine

"You should win an Olympic medal. You really should." Dylan looked at her with something approaching awe. "I had no idea anyone could shop like that. It was like you were dancing."

"And you kept up with me. Colour me impressed. Think I got enough?"

The back of the car was filled with bags and boxes of varying sizes. "More than enough."

"And it was all on sale! My mother always told me to never pay full price for anything if I could help it."

"I can't believe you got all this and only spent two-hundred dollars. If a man bought a car load of stuff, it would cost him thousands."

"That's because men don't know how to shop," Rebecca said.

"So I've learned tonight."

"What would you like to do now? I wish I had picked up that necklace though, too bad the mall is closing. Nine o'clock comes far too early! I think malls should stay open until eleven at the very least, that way—"

Dylan leaned in to kiss her. He didn't plan it, there was just something so wonderful about her that he had to find out what it felt like to press his lips against hers. Dylan expected her to resist, to pull back and tell him to stop, but she surprised him by leaning in and kissing him back.

It was soft at first, as if she were hesitant and unsure, but soon the kissing grew heavy and heated. Dylan wrapped his arms around her to pull her closer, so that he could feel all of her pressed against him. He could feel her heart beat and it was going just as fast as his was.

Finally, she drew back slowly, as if afraid to end the kiss or the moment of contact between them. He looked into her eyes to find that they were a deep and gorgeous blue. He could get lost in those eyes, lost in her. Dylan already was.

Rebecca ran a hand along his cheek, touching him as if afraid he would disappear. "Woah," she said.

"Woah."

"You kiss way better than your brother."

Dylan didn't know what he was expecting her to say, but it wasn't this. Instead of getting angry though, he started to laugh. His laughter bubbled up from the pit of his stomach and wouldn't be stopped. It rippled out of him and soon, Rebecca was laughing right along with him. They both laughed until they had tears running down their faces.

When Dylan could actually breathe, he said, "You kissed Devon?"

"Yeah." She hiccupped and smiled. "It was one night a few years ago. We were both drunk and were both bemoaning the fact that we were both alone and lonely."

"That's the same thing."

"No, it's not. You can be with someone and be alone. You can be alone but not be lonely because you have friends surrounding you. So, we got talking and then he looked at me and said 'We could get together, you know?' I was like, 'But you're gay.' Still though, we ended up kissing on his couch, then never spoke of it again."

"So, how am I better?" Dylan asked with a grin.

"Devon used his tongue a lot and kept biting my lips and shit. You could tell he kissed a lot of men because a woman doesn't like to be covered in saliva. It was kind of nasty. Now I'm sure that's all good to go for the gays, but I like a kisser who is gentle and lets the fire build, you know?" She reached up and touched his lips. "You, on the other hand, are all fire underneath your skin. You know how to kiss like a gentleman."

Dylan tried to think of something to say to that, but in the end, he just started kissing her, seeing if he could stoke the fire within them both.

Chapter Sixty

Gaston took her to an all-night diner. Apparently, they served the best eggs in the world. They sat across from each other eating, talking, and just enjoying one another's company. It felt so good to laugh with someone, to learn more about his life and to fall a little bit more in love with him.

While she was freshening up in the washroom, Romilda realized she had never really dated anyone. Sure, she and Cordellia had dated a little, then they got married and had Blaine together. But as a woman, Romilda hadn't dated anyone. She had been on a few blind dates and she had been honest up front about her being trans. The guy usually just got up from the table in disgust and left her with the check.

So, she had stopped trying to find love, had waited for it to find her. But after more than fifteen years, she had stopped waiting. Love wasn't meant for her, she had decided. Romilda had worked on repairing the relationship that she had with Cordellia. It was the closest thing she had to a stable relationship, so she chose to cherish it.

In the end, she began to wonder if she hadn't tried to date more because she was afraid of falling in love, of losing herself in someone else when it had taken so long to find who she was. She had built walls to keep others out, even patrons at the GLBTQ Library. Some of them had hit on her but she had always put the kibosh on that. She wondered if there had been one other thing that had kept her away from love.

When she came back to the table, it was to find that Gaston had ordered them glasses of red wine. She raised her right eyebrow. "Wine at a diner?"

"Hey, they sell good stuff. Think of this as the pre-dessert drink. I'm going to take you to a lovely place that sells cake to die for. This is just the appetizer."

"You do know how to spoil an old lady."

"Oh honey, there is nothing old about you. You've got a young soul, so that makes all of you young."

"I'm near seventy. That's old."

"No, Romy, that's just the beginning." He held up his glass. "To the beginning."

"Of what?"

Gaston gave her a wicked grin. "Of us."

Romilda blushed and clinked her glass against his. Then she took a sip and was surprised by how wonderful it tasted. It was light and fruity one moment and soft as silk the next. "This is very good wine!"

"I'm glad you approve."

"I have something to say to you, Gaston. I will probably ramble it out in a rush, but I need to say this, okay? Will you listen?"

"I always listen to you. Your voice is like music to me."

Blushing, Romilda gathered her thoughts. She knew the best place to begin was at the beginning, so she started there. "For the longest time, I've been afraid of myself."

Gaston took her hand. "Whatever do you mean?"

"I've been afraid of what I needed to become. Too many people were so freaked out by how I 'used to be a man' that I started to get freaked out myself. It's been easier to hide in the dark rather than to actively find love."

"You have nothing to be afraid of with me, you know that, right?"

"I do. But what I'm saying is that I've been afraid of myself, treating myself as if I'm made of eggshells and liable to break. I had a thought when I was in the washroom."

"I do some of my best thinking in washrooms. It's why I always bring a book to read while I'm busy."

Letting out a laugh, Romilda looked at Gaston, really looked at him. All she saw was kindness and light. It seemed as if he had a halo, the light from him was so bright. Of course, that might be the pot light above his head, but you couldn't blame a girl for romanticizing.

"I am pretty sure that I could fall in love with you," she said. "I don't want to be afraid anymore, of you or myself. I'm done being afraid."

"Babe, that's music to my ears. Finish up your wine and we can go and get that cake. And perhaps a little more wine."

Chapter Sixty-One

Curtis had been right, the pancakes at Talia's were indeed to die for. Devon had ordered the spinach and mushroom omelette and had never tasted better.

Over food and coffee, they chatted. Devon was pretty sure he had never actually talked to any of the men he had been with aside from Nancy, and there had always been drama with Nancy. That was just his style.

With Curtis, the conversation flowed easily, and it was drama-free. He had never met a man like him. Curtis was funny and kind and genuine. A man could get used to this, he thought.

"What's that smile you're wearing for? I'm telling you about the horrors of dealing with aunts who still try to set you up with a woman, and you're not reacting in horror. You should be afraid, 'cause if I ever introduce you to my aunt Eloise, she'll say she knows just the lady friend for you to meet, even though she'll know you're gay."

"I'm smiling because of you. You don't know how nice it is to have an actual conversation with a guy."

"You've been with lots of guys, surely you had conversations with them?"

"Yeah, but it amounted to laying out ground work like no kissing, no glove no love, and did they want to be the top or the bottom?"

"Oh, you can swing either way? That'll be fun."

There was a twinkle in Curtis's eye that sent Devon's heart racing. He was pretty sure his cheeks reddened, and that was another first.

"You're very cute when you blush, you know. But why are

you so nervous? I don't make you nervous, do I?"

"If you did, would I have answered the door buck naked?"

"True. Then why are you blushing?"

"Because I've never cared what another person thought of me."

"What about Nancy?"

Sighing, Devon took another sip of coffee before he answered. "It was all about me then. Sure, I loved him, but not completely. I didn't give him all of my heart. You know? Does that even make sense?"

"Sure, it does. You were so used to keeping part of your heart under lock and key."

"But I loved him."

"Not completely, otherwise, it wouldn't have been just about you. It would have been about the two of you."

Devon shook his head. "I don't even know why you're talking to me."

Curtis reached across the table and took his free hand. "Because I see you as the man you're trying to be. I wouldn't have even talked to you if you had still been hooking."

"But I was so cruel to him."

"I get that. But you grieved. People learn and grow a lot when they grieve. I know that you're a different person now that you went through the dark forest."

"The dark forest? Like with a Wicked Witch and what not?"

"Wrong story, but same forest."

A laugh bubbled out of Devon's mouth. It started out slowly but then built to full force with little warning. Chuckling that had turned into big belly laughs. Soon, Curtis was laughing with him.

When the laughter stopped, Devon realized he was

holding on to Curtis's hand with both of his. Devon had never felt so whole, so complete and wondered if it was all to do with Curtis.

Curtis leaned forward and kissed him softly on the lips, sending a thrill of heat all the way down Devon's body. Curtis smiled and whispered, "Let me pay the bill."

"We're leaving?"

"I don't think Talia would appreciate it if I took you right now on the table. Plus, that would be murder on my back."

Chapter Sixty-Two

Rebecca had to keep reminding herself that Dylan wasn't Devon.

She could see a lot of resemblance between the two of them, but throughout the day and the evening, she learned that Dylan was a kinder, gentler version of Devon. Devon stored his heart in a locked box, probably from being burned so many times. He hid it behind bravado and drama.

Dylan, on the other hand, was confident and self-aware but wasn't cocky about it. Instead, Rebecca could see kindness in every gesture. And confident kindness was a really big turn-on for her.

They were walking on the pier, down near the water. The stars were out, and she and Dylan were even holding hands. She couldn't remember the last time she had held hands with a man. It had probably been Devon, but that didn't count. Sure, he was a man, but she would never get Devon into bed.

"What are you thinking?" Dylan asked.

"Huh?"

"Well, you look lost in thought. What are you thinking about?"

She sighed and looked at him, really looked at him. She saw every laugh line and potential wrinkle on his face. Dylan's face was so different than Devon's. Devon had no laugh lines whatsoever. That had more to do with the botox he got as opposed to an absence of a sense of humour. "I was just thinking."

"I know you were. You were about to walk off the pier."

She looked down at her feet and saw that she was right on the edge of the wood. The next step would have brought her into the water. "So I was. Thank you for saving me."

"And they say that chivalry is dead. Really, what's up with you?"

Taking a deep breath, Rebecca reminded herself that she wasn't invested yet, not really. What existed between them was the potential of something, the spark that started a fire. Nothing more. "I've been in love with your brother for a long time."

Dylan took in a shocked breath. "Man, I was afraid you were going to tell me you were a lesbian. I wasn't expecting that."

She smacked him playfully. "Would a lesbian shop like that?"

"I don't know; you'll have to ask them."

"I'm being serious here. I love your brother but recently figured out for myself that nothing would ever happen between him and me, not the way I wanted it to."

"I see the problem. He's gay, you're straight. That could cause an issue. You love him? Like really love him?"

"I do...but have been working hard on loving him as a friend and not a potential lover. They always say the fag hag really loves the man, but I always thought that was a joke, you know? I didn't think I'd be another one of the stereotypical hags that end up loving a man who can never love her back."

Dylan put both of his hands on her shoulders and leaned in closer. She could smell something citrusy and bright, so unlike Devon's scent. "First of all, you are not a hag. You are one of the most beautiful women I have ever seen. Secondly, it's okay to love someone who can't love you back that way, so stop beating yourself up about it."

He ran a thumb along her lips and leaned in to kiss them. Rebecca breathed him in.

"You can't help who you love, but I hope you're not freaking out because we're brothers. I might look like him, but I'm nothing like him."

"I'm beginning to realize that."

"Good, that's good. We can work on loving each other. In the meantime, let's continue our walk. The stars don't shine just for anyone, you know."

She held his hand and walked on with Dylan a bit. Finally, smiling, she said, "Just because I could fall in love with you doesn't mean I'm changing your name on my cell phone."

Chapter Sixty-Three

On the drive over to The Cabin, Chuck thought it would be a good time to talk to Sebastian.

He had received three more calls on his cell phone and each time they had ended the same way. Sebastian would pretend like nothing had happened, as if he hadn't just yelled at whoever was on the other end of the telephone. Chuck was worried about Sebastian and who might be on the other end of the phone.

Chuck was driving. They drove in silence for a little bit until Sebastian asked, "So, what's going on with William?"

"I'm not sure. Nancy just said to meet at The Cabin for an emergency meeting. Poppy and Dava will be there as well as Justin and Blaine. Mike is coming with Nancy."

"It has been too long since we've all gotten together."

"What do you mean? We did a group thing last week!"

"Exactly, a week is like a month in gay time."

"Touché."

"Why are Mike and William talking anyway? William was horrible to him."

"Well, would you stop talking to me if we ever broke up?"

"No, 'cause we're not going to break up."

"I know that, but how could you just cut a person you loved from your life?"

"Easy, you move on when they hurt you."

"Not every relationship ends that way."

"True. But sometimes it's just too painful to talk to that person. Even though they were a part of your life, it might hurt too much."

"Is that what happened with the person who keeps calling you?"

The silence this time was glacial. When Sebastian spoke this time, the tone was carefully nonchalant. "What person?"

"The person who keeps calling you. You keep yelling at them and hanging up on them."

"I don't know what you're talking about."

"Sebastian," Chuck spoke in his don't-fuck-with-me voice, "I'm not stupid. I know someone's been calling you."

"I don't want to talk about this now."

"What, you'll tell me you used to be a woman, but you won't tell me about who this person is? It can't be that bad."

"This is different. I don't want to have this conversation."

"You always said there would be no secrets between us. Now there's this person! Why can't you tell me?"

"It's not that I can't. It's that I don't want to. Not yet."

Concentrating on the road, Chuck said nothing. He didn't know what to say. Chuck almost jumped when Sebastian reached out and placed a hand on Chuck's leg.

"I'm sorry. I will tell you. I promise I will. I'm just not ready yet. It hurts too much, and I just want to focus on the good thing that we're building. But I will tell you."

Chuck pulled into the parking lot for The Cabin and turned off the car. He turned his head to look at Sebastian. "It had better be soon," he said and got out of the car.

Chapter Sixty-Four

Nancy was in his element.

Everyone had arrived. To help a friend out, sure, but still they came. That showed him that this group was strong no matter what happened. Nancy welcomed everyone as they headed towards the group. A hostess's job was never done.

"Chucky Cheese! Sebastian! You made it!"

"He gets called his real name and I get Chucky Cheese again. Why can't I just be Chuck?"

"Okay, you can be Chuck and Sebastian can be Peppermint Patty," Nancy said.

"Nah, stick with Chucky Cheese." Sebastian was grinning ear to ear.

"Bastard," Chuck said.

Nancy looked at them and marvelled that, through everything, they had stuck together. They were like a family, and it was growing. Blaine sat with Justin, Mike beside them with an empty spot for Nancy. William sat next to Poppy's left side and Dava was on her right.

"What are we doing here, exactly?" Chuck looked at William and tried not to sneer. "Are we talking to you now?"

"We're here to help him, in whatever way we can. William is in trouble and you help your friends when they're in trouble," Nancy said. "Don't make me give you the same talking to that I gave Mike. Don't make me whoop your ass."

"What'll you do, beat me with your high-heeled shoe?"

"Honey they're five inches. I will cut you."

"What's going on?" Blaine asked. He turned to William. He looked worse for wear. There were bruises on his face and lacerations on his hands. "Are you okay?"

William shook his head and the tears started to fall. They slid down his cheeks and into his beer. "No, I'm not okay. I've done something terribly stupid. Something I don't know how to get out of."

Blaine gave Nancy a wide-eyed look. "He's being beaten by David," Nancy stated.

Everyone sucked in a breath. Blaine paled, and Poppy leaned over to hug William. Chuck looked abashed. "Shit, I'm sorry dude."

"I don't know what to do! He tracked down Blaine when he wanted him back. I'm afraid that he'll find me and come after me."

"Let's not forget what David did to Devon when Devon wouldn't do what he wanted." Chuck said.

"Let's also not forget that Devon is an asshole," Justin said.

"That's beside the point. We protect our own," said Nancy. "We have to stand up to him. We just have to. He's hurt three people we know, and we can't let it happen again."

"What do you suggest we do?" Dava asked.

"I'm going to call Cordellia tomorrow morning. See if it would be okay with her if William hid out at her place. I don't think David would be stupid enough to mess with her."

"I'll call her," Blaine said. "I'm sure she'd be fine with it, and Justin and I could stay there, too, just to make sure nothing happens."

"So, that's decided. But what do we do about David?" Mike asked. "I mean, I beat the shit out of him, but he'll be back."

"I think you're all forgetting who my ex-girlfriend is," Poppy said.

"What, Connie or The River Flows Through It?" Chuck said with a smile.

"You know perfectly well that the name she prefers is River Moon Falls." She laughed out loud. "You can be such an asshole, but that's a good one. Still, she's a twisted bitch and will give as good as she gets. She'll take him down."

"I'll help," Justin said. "I don't do much personal law anymore, mostly property. But we can get a peace bond and a restraining order. I can put something together that's iron clad."

William looked at all of them, the tears finally stopping. His eyes looked like glass and it was as if one swift breeze would break him into shards. "Thank you. Thank you, so much. I don't deserve your help."

"Yes, you do," Dava said. "You made a mistake. There's no reason you should pay for it for the rest of your life. We got you."

"Now that that's settled, let's get this guy a beer, one for each hand!" Chuck said.

Chapter Sixty-Five

Devon was in shock.

Curtis sat propped up against the headboard, having a cigarette. The smoke made curls that reached towards the ceiling, almost as if it were dancing. "So," he said. "Was it good for you?"

Looking at him, Devon saw Curtis wearing a wide grin like the Cheshire Cat. Sweat was still slick on their bodies and Devon's heart was thumping. "It was better than good. I'm pretty sure you're an angel."

"Oh, Devon, an angel wouldn't have been able to pull off what we just did, not even with wings to levitate."

"How did you learn to do that?"

"Which part?" Curtis asked. "The part where you had your legs on either side of my head or the backwards reach-around bit that made you sound like you were praying?"

"Both."

"A gentleman never tells his secrets." Stubbing out the cigarette, Curtis leaned closer and kissed him. "Why so quiet? You look like the cat got your tongue, or something. Is anything wrong?"

"No, nothing's wrong. I just had the best sex of my life, that's all. I want to shout about it from the rooftops, actually."

"You don't want to make all those people who aren't getting any jealous. If you're so happy, why are you so quiet?"

Devon lit his own cigarette to give him time to find the words. He wasn't sure what to say but finally just let the words out. "I thought I knew all about sex. I knew about fucking, sucking, touching. But I didn't know about this, not at all. I had no idea, I didn't even have this with Nancy."

Curtis raised an eyebrow and gave him a wry look. "Wow, you sure cleared that up for me, thanks." Laughing, Curtis said, "You'll have to be a lot clearer than that, handsome."

Devon shook his head. "I thought I knew it all, but I didn't know anything like this. With one tumble in the hay, you've reshaped everything."

"Gosh, you're cute when you're confusing. You get this little dimple in your left cheek when you try to be serious."

"I'm trying to tell you something!"

"So, tell me."

Devon took a breath and began again. "I was a hooker for crying out loud. Sex was my job. But along the way, it lost the magic for me. It became a way to get off, a way to get paid. It was just a means to an end. I didn't love anyone I slept with, not even Nancy, not completely. Why did tonight mean more to me than the hundreds of other times I got laid?"

"Well, it's really simple, actually." Curtis ran a fingertip along Devon's chest, making him shiver. "It was about more than just your cock and balls, which are fantastic, by the way. It was about your heart."

"Are you talking about love?"

"I'm talking about the possibility of love, about emotion. You were one cold horse while you were cruising around looking for your next customer. Now you've mellowed out a bit and you've learned from having a broken heart, or from breaking someone else's."

"I remember feeling this way after sex, a long time ago."

"Oh now, it's only been ten minutes! I know gay time moves quickly, but you have to give a man a moment to breathe!"

Curtis took one look at Devon's shocked face and laughed. "Oh, come here handsome. Let's see if we can go for round two."

Chapter Sixty-Six

The morning had come too early. William and Nancy had gone out to get some of William's stuff and to see if Cordellia was home so that Nancy could talk to her. He figured the human approach was better than a telephone call.

Justin was enjoying a bit of quiet time, getting the paperwork ready for William's peace bond. Justin knew that the bond wouldn't amount to much if David meant business, but it couldn't hurt. Every little thing they could do for him would help. It just had to.

He was so consumed in the paperwork, he almost didn't hear the knock. Turning to look at the door, Justin wondered who it could be this early in the morning. It was barely past nine o'clock.

Walking towards the door, he was suddenly filled with a sense of unease. It was as if his body didn't want him to answer the door, and he stopped in mid step. "Just being silly," he said out loud. Shaking it off, he reached for the doorknob and opened it…then felt the world fall out from under him.

Standing in the doorway was his mother.

"Good morning, son. I trust I'm not keeping you from anything?"

"Actually, I'm working on something." He tried to keep the coldness out of his voice but wasn't entirely successful.

"Surely your own mother is more important than whatever you were working on. Aren't you going to invite me in for a cup of tea?"

Justin crossed his arms and tried not to glare at his mother but again was unsuccessful. "What are you doing here, Mother?"

She gave a huff of breath that reeked of disapproval. "Can't we discuss this inside your apartment? I don't want your neighbours talking."

Holding back a groan, Justin let her into the apartment and closed the door. He turned to find his mother inspecting everything, taking it all in with something approaching approval. She eyed Blaine's art with care, going up to one canvas and staring at it longer than all the rest.

"Who is this artist?" she asked. Victoria was an avid art collector and she only bought the ones that spoke to her. Also, the ones that were worth millions of dollars. "The brushwork is incredible. Such emotion, such depth! I'm glad to see you got my taste in art at the very least."

Justin smirked. "That's one of Blaine's."

"Your…friend? Well, then I must find out where he got it."

"Blaine didn't buy it. He did it."

"Your friend painted this? Really?"

"Mother, he's not my friend. He's my partner and my soon-to-be husband."

"Now, really," Victoria crossed her arms and came closer to him. "Can you people even do that nowadays?"

"Yes, we can and you know it. Equal marriage has been legal for over a decade. Don't you remember how shocked you were when it happened? You couldn't sleep for a week, worrying over the state of what the world had become."

"Son, you have to understand, we come from another generation."

"Don't give me that crap! All you needed to do was love me and accept me. Why was that so hard for you?"

Victoria let out another huff of breath that was quickly followed by a small groan. "Oh, Justin. I'm making a mess of

144

this. Can I get a cup of tea and start over?"

Justin was moved to see that his mother's eyes were glassy with unshed tears. His mother never got emotional. She never cried. There was a reason that he called her the ice princess; nothing got to her, ever.

"Sure, Mother. What kind of tea would you like?"

"Orange Pekoe if you have it. Earl Grey if you don't."

"We have both. Blaine got me on to drinking tea. I prefer herbal tea myself."

Victoria huffed. "That's hardly tea. That's just flavoured water."

Justin laughed at that and looked at his mother with shock. "Did you just make a joke? You never joke, Mother."

"There are a lot of things you don't know about me, Justin."

"I have yet to see that, but I'm willing to let you show me."

He boiled the water and made two cups of tea, an Orange Pekoe for her and an Earl Grey for him. "There you go, Mother."

"Thank you."

"So, talk. You came here to tell me something, now is your chance to say it."

Victoria took a sip of tea and then put the mug down. "I wanted to reach out to you. I don't want to lose you, Justin. You're my only son, my baby boy. I want to have a relationship with you again."

She took another sip of tea and slowly put the cup down. "Also, I've left your father. I need a place to stay for a few days until I can get myself in order. My things will arrive here tomorrow."

Justin spat out his tea.

Chapter Sixty-Seven

Sebastian was in heaven.

Well, as close to it as he could get. He was living with the man of his dreams and they were building a home together. He had been accepted by Chuck's friends and felt like he had a family again. Sebastian had taken the day off work to set up more of the apartment, wanting to surprise Chuck when he got home.

Chuck had gone with Nancy and Blaine to talk to Nan about William. Mike was watching William and who knew what Poppy would tell River Moon Falls, AKA Connie. Shaking his head, Sebastian smiled and wondered how his life had gotten so full of so many people. It had just been himself for a long time until he met Chuck.

Sebastian was finishing the hanging of some pictures when there was a knock on his door. As he went to answer it, he had a feeling in the pit of his stomach. It froze his legs to the floor. He didn't know who was on the other side of that door, but something was telling him not to answer it.

He shook that off, not one to believe in superstitions and premonitions, and walked towards the door. When he opened it, he felt his stomach drop to the ground.

Standing there was a girl. She was tall and too thin, had red hair and sparkling green eyes. She gave him a small smile. "Hi, Mom."

"Cassandra," Sebastian whispered. "Cassandra, what are you doing here?"

"Well, you would know that if you talked to Dad on the phone, wouldn't you? You haven't taken any of his calls, so I just decided enough with this bullshit and came on down myself."

"How did you find out where I lived?"

She rolled her eyes at him. "Google, duh. You can find anything on the internet. You must know that. Now, are you going to invite me in, or am I just going to stand here looking pretty?"

"I told Kyle that I didn't want to talk to him."

"Yeah, but I'm what he wanted to talk to you about."

Cassandra brushed past Sebastian and dropped her bags in the doorway, closing the door behind her. "Got any food? It was a long trip and I'm starving."

"Sweetie, this isn't a good time."

"It hasn't been a good time for you for, like, ten years. Ten years, dude. I'm legal now and everything!"

"So?"

"So, while you're rustling up some food, how about a glass of wine?"

"Oh, no. Absolutely not."

"You lost the right to tell me what to do when you left. It's been ten years. I haven't seen you in ten years. I need a glass of wine." Cassandra crossed her arms in front of her chest.

Sebastian thought he was going to lose it. In front of him stood his daughter, the one he thought he would never have to see when he began his life again. Now, here she was, loud as life and demanding a glass of alcohol.

"Okay," he said, finally. "So do I."

"He speaks sense! My mom is awesome," Cassandra said sarcastically.

Sighing, Sebastian took down two wine glasses and was about to open a bottle of red wine when the door opened. Chuck walked in and took a look at Cassandra surrounded by all of her luggage and then turned to look at Sebastian.

"Who's she?" he asked.

"I'm his daughter," Cassandra said before Sebastian could respond. "Who the fuck are you?"

Chapter Sixty-Eight

William gazed at Cordellia's face and saw only pity there.

All the time he had known her, she had looked upon him with kindness, mirth, and with love—but never pity. He stayed silent while Nan took everything in, and he wished she would change her expression.

"So, we need to keep him somewhere safe," Nancy finished explaining. "Somewhere where he won't be out in the open and where David can't find him."

"And you thought of my place?" Cordellia asked.

"Well sure, David has never been here. He doesn't know where you live," Nancy said.

"If David is smart enough to find Blaine at his place of work, then surely he can find William here."

"We just need to keep him safe. We're asking for your help with that," Blaine said.

"Funny, you're doing all the talking, but William doesn't seem able to say anything."

William shrivelled a little bit but there was still a bit of pride within him, a small kernel of light that shone despite the darkness he currently found himself in. "Look, I screwed up, okay? I royally fucked the pooch on this one. I knew what he was, who he was, when I took up with him. I was so mad at Mike, so mad at myself for wanting someone else at the same time I wanted Mike. I screwed up and let someone fuck me up. At the time I thought I deserved it. Now I know I don't."

William finally looked up and looked at Cordellia right in the eyes. "Judge me however you want to, but I'm asking for your help. Please."

Cordellia stared at him and didn't say anything. Finally,

they watched as her face softened, and she reached out a hand to place it on his cheek. "You poor boy. You poor, brave boy. Of course, I'll help you. Of course, I will. You can call my house your house for as long as you need to. Until that rat bastard is in jail or someone helps him kick the bucket."

"Cordellia!" Mike blurted, aware that William was shocked by her anger, too.

"I mean it. You don't put someone down because you're too small. You don't spit on someone because you're too stupid. And you certainly don't hit someone because you're afraid of yourself, so you have to hit others to feel better about yourself."

She was riled now and went to the fridge, taking out some pink lemonade. "We need a drink."

"I'm okay, Cordellia," Nancy said.

"Well, I'm not. And you're all having a drink with me."

Cordellia took down a bottle of vodka from one of the kitchen cupboards and poured a generous shot into each of the three glasses. Nancy looked aghast.

"Cordellia! It's only ten o'clock in the morning!"

"Mom, it's too early to drink alcohol. How about some coffee?" Blaine said.

"It's beer o'clock somewhere in the world," Cordellia retorted.

"Yes, but we're having vodka and lemonade," William pointed out.

"Shut up and drink your medicine."

All four of them lifted their glasses and clinked. "To your health," Nancy said.

"To growing a spine," William sighed.

"To getting stronger!" Blaine grinned.

"To small dicks!" Cordellia added.

William burst out laughing. "What brought that on?"

She took a chug of her drink, then let out a heavy sigh. "I'm sorry dears, I just get so riled up when something happens to someone like this. Especially to one of my boys. Men who have small dicks are usually the angriest, haven't you ever noticed? So, if we send him a bit of cheer, maybe he won't be upset about that."

"He'll still be an asshole," William said.

"Yes, he will dear. He's an abuser. They don't know any other way. When I think of what that man did to my sweet Blaine…" She let out another sigh. "You're safe here William. I'll make sure of it. If it comes to it, Romilda can run guard duty."

"Romilda? What will she be able to do?"

"Oh, she kicked David's ass before, and he's not likely to forget that. If he should pop by for a visit, maybe he'll need a reminder that a woman kicked his sorry ass." She smiled at them. "Drink up, boys. It won't drink itself, you know."

Chapter Sixty-Nine

Poppy thought of how to talk to Dava.

She had wanted to say something for days now about the subject of Dava's husband but couldn't find the words. Dava seemed unwilling to discuss the matter at all.

After the mad dash from his place, when they had driven away to the sound of broken bottles hitting the pavement, Dava had been pale and shaken. Poppy couldn't blame her, Poppy would have been terrified—had been terrified.

Poppy wanted to give Dava time to make up her own mind and her own decision, but she hadn't said anything. Instead, Dava had talked about how awful William was, how horrible that he had been involved with David, and what it was doing to all of them.

That was the last straw for Poppy. She had to say something. Despite her better judgement, she felt the words pouring out of her mouth without a hope to stop them. "Then why don't you feel horrible about your situation?"

Dava looked at her with a raised eyebrow. "Me? I'm perfectly happy. I have you in my life and we're building a life together. What's horrible about that?"

Poppy looked at her with disbelief. "Seriously? You don't see any parallels between yourself and William?"

"I don't know what you mean."

"God, do I have to spell it out for you? William is being terrorized by an abusive man. You can't tell me that you don't see the similarities."

"I don't, actually. I got away from that life. I left Fred behind, got myself and my boys out of there, and started a new life, the life I always wanted. It led me to you. How is that remotely the same as what David is doing to William?"

Poppy poured a cup of decaf coffee for her and regular coffee for Dava and came into the living room to sit beside her. Handing Dava her cup, Poppy tried to remember that this wasn't her life and to remain calm. "It's the same because you're still afraid of him. We drove away so fast from him that I'm surprised the transmission didn't fall out."

"And what would you have had me do? You saw how he was, didn't you?" Putting down her cup of coffee, Dava wrung her hands in her lap. "I got away with my life and my boys are safe. That should be enough, shouldn't it?"

"It should be, but he's still a part of your life as long as you're married to him. How long has it been anyway?"

"Almost ten years, ten glorious years."

"Why did you drive me out there?"

"What do you mean?"

"I mean, why did we go out there if we weren't going to do anything?"

"I wanted to see if I could face him and stand up to him. If I could be brave enough to tell him that I wanted a divorce."

"You do?"

"Of course, I do! I want to be married to you with every fibre of my being! I want to build a real life with you, heart and soul. But I'm too afraid of him, Poppy! I'm so afraid of him. I still dream about what he used to do to me, the slaps and the punches he used to give me if everything wasn't the right way."

Poppy put down her own cup of coffee and took Dava's hands in her own. "You never told me what it was like with him. I had no idea."

"It's not a chapter of my life that I want to relive."

"The chapter is still going as long as you're married to him, Dava. Besides which, you have me. I'll support you. And

153

the boys will take care of you. Cordellia and Romilda, too. You're not alone. We've all dealt with our share of assholes. Being afraid is nothing to be ashamed of."

Poppy was silenced by the tears running down Dava's face. They streaked her cheeks like rain and Dava did nothing to wipe them away. "¬I'm so afraid he'll come after me like David did to Blaine, putting you in danger. I don't know what I would do if that happened. I would die if he hurt you."

Poppy pulled Dava into an embrace and just held her. She let Dava cry it out and rubbed her back, the whole time her entire heart and soul ached for this beautiful woman. "You listen to me, Dava. Nothing will happen to me or to you. You're the bravest person I've ever loved. You ran from danger, protected your children and yourself against all odds. You will beat him, too. We will find a way and I will be beside you the entire time. That's a promise."

Dava sat up and looked at Poppy. Dava's eyes were puffy and red but she gave Poppy a weak smile. "I'm not brave."

"You are if I say you are. I'll talk to Justin and see if there's something we can do. In the meantime, dry your eyes. We're going out."

"Out? Where?"

"To find you a mimosa and the non-alcoholic alternative for me and then go for a walk to look at something lovely. Life is too beautiful to be cooped up inside today. Okay?"

Leaning forward to kiss Poppy softly on the lips, Dava gave her a real smile. "Okay."

Chapter Seventy

Rebecca wondered what she was going to do with her day.

After the marathon shopping spree with Dylan, she didn't need to go shopping. Who was she kidding? She could always shop. It helped to fill a void. She wondered when the void had started.

She supposed it had begun when she knew Devon would never be capable of loving her. So, Rebecca bought things, trinkets, clothes, and shoes. They would always love me and not ask questions…right? She had hated shopping as a child and yet, she had become one of those women that had to have the latest purse and the newest hard-to-find shoes—not that there was anything wrong with that.

What was the problem then? It had been bothering Rebecca for some time and she had finally realized that she was filling a void. She didn't have the love that she wanted, so she filled it with things that didn't require an emotional attachment. She had friends, sure, but she didn't see them very often. She had her job as an editor for a company that published political magazines, boring work, but it paid well.

What bothered Rebecca the most was that she had become one of those women she hated most. The kind of who lusted after a man she couldn't have and tried to fill her life with things that she loved instead. She might have had only a handful of friends, but she had a closet filled with purses, shoes, and jewellery. She could open her own store, for fuck's sake.

Walking into her closet, she looked at all the things she had bought instead of letting a man into her life, except the guy who she knew could not love her the way she wanted. She had never once tried allowing someone else in.

She remembered as a girl, dreaming of the man she would love. He had been modeled off Prince Charming, but that was beside the point. When did she become afraid of love, of letting people love her? Her parents had passed away years ago and she was an only child, but here she was at twenty-nine, alone. How had she let that happen?

She had spent too many nights sitting by herself watching romantic comedies on television, her tub of Häagen-Dazs close by. She had spent too many days filled up to the brim with something to do rather than getting to know people. And then there was Devon. She knew she had to let him go, that she could still be friends with him, the best of friends. But she could never love him that way and he would never love her.

Rebecca wondered why it was his brother Dylan who had somehow showed her the right way. Yes, he was another man, and she had to give him a fair shot. Something was happening between them. Rather than running away, flailing her arms and screaming, she would instead open them wide and welcome Dylan into her life. She was ready.

Her phone rang. Looking at the readout, she saw 'I'm an asshole' on the phone and knew who it would be. She found herself smiling when she pressed accept and said, "Hello, Dylan."

"Why, you sound happy to hear from me. No witty remarks or sarcastic hellos?"

She giggled and wondered when she had really laughed. "Nope. I've missed you."

"It's been less than a day. Better be careful or that could become contagious."

"Why, did you miss me?"

"Yes, as a matter of fact, I did. What are you doing right now?"

"Looking at my collection of stuff and wondering when I started replacing the people in my life with purses and shoes."

"Sounds philosophical. Fancy going for breakfast to wow me with your deep insights?"

"Sure. When?"

"Can you be ready in fifteen?"

"Make it twenty minutes, and we have a deal."

"See you then."

She clicked off the phone and was surprised to find herself smiling. *God, it feels good. I should try doing it more often, starting now.*

Chapter Seventy-One

Romilda had never spent so much time with a man.

There had been men in her life, back when she was still a man. Back when she had thought she was gay and hadn't fully admitted to herself who she was, what she held inside of her. No relationship had ever lasted because she wasn't being true to herself.

In truth, she had never spent time with herself either. Sure, she did what she had to do to become who she was meant to be, but when was the last time she had spent a quiet moment with herself? When had she stopped listening to herself and what she wanted out of life?

The truth was that she wanted Gaston with all of her heart. Romilda wanted him, all of him, pure and simple. But then again, matters of the heart were never that easy. They were messy and catastrophic and glorious and wonderful. She had to stop thinking and get busy living, otherwise it would pass her by in an instant.

Romilda had spent too much of her life hiding what she wanted, what she needed. That would have to end, too. Gaston was a breath of fresh air; he revitalized her, and she was not afraid of what would happen.

These thoughts ran through her head as she watched him sleep. They had spent last night together, and it had been beautiful. They hadn't made love; they merely talked. She couldn't remember the last time she had spoken so much with a man. Hell, with anyone. He wanted to know all about her life and what had brought her here, to this moment.

Looking at him, she took in the dark hair with grey and white strands threaded throughout, the strong jawline and those kissable lips that she loved so much. She knew what the rest of him looked like, and the memory of that sent a thrill through her.

Gaston opened his eyes. "Honey, you're thinking so loud."

"Well, good morning to you, too."

He smiled brightly at her. "Good morning, gorgeous."

"Are you saying that thinking is a bad thing?"

"This early in the morning without coffee? Yes, it is. And you're thinking so loudly I'm surprised that the neighbours next-door or down the street can't here you. Honey, when was the last time you just relaxed?"

"I'm too tightly wound up to relax."

"I've noticed. I know what we're going to do today."

"What did you have in mind?"

"We're going to go do something that helps you relax."

Romilda smiled wickedly. "I can think of a few things."

Letting out a laugh, Gaston pulled her down onto the bed beside him. "I just bet you can. Well, then after that. What makes you the happiest?"

"Besides you? You're going to think it's silly."

"Nothing you do is silly."

"Well I have to work in the library today. It's the place where I'm happiest."

"The library?"

"Sure, surrounded by all those books and all that knowledge? Stories waiting to be read, books just crying out to be picked up and held for hours on end? Characters waiting to form a bond with a reader who will love them forever? What's not to love about that?"

Gaston kissed her then, deeply and without holding back anything. Normally, he had been gentle, as if he was afraid that she would break and fall apart. Now, it was as if he were

159

delving into her. Romilda kissed him back just as completely.

When they broke apart, Gaston looked into her eyes as he placed a hand on either side of her head. "I love you Romy," he said. "I love you with all my heart."

Chapter Seventy-Two

He had to admit it, waking up next to Devon had been like the stuff dreams are made of.

Sure, Curtis had seen him around, always cruising the bar. He had always looked past Curtis, as if he wasn't worth the time or didn't have the money. Running into Devon at the bar the other night had been pure happenstance.

He had carried a minor flame for Devon for a while, all the men in the gay community had. Devon was tall, well built, had deep dark eyes and gorgeous dark hair. He was almost every gay man's dreamboat.

Curtis couldn't believe it when Devon had started talking to him. It was as if he had won some sort of sex lottery. For a minute or two, Curtis couldn't believe someone that good-looking would take the time to speak to someone like him.

At that moment, his best friend Sasha's voice rang out in his head: "Sweetie, you got junk in the trunk and gold in your heart. Everything else is just window dressing."

It had taken a long time for Curtis to love himself. He had never fit the image of the hot gay man, whatever that was. He was shorter than most guys and about thirty pounds overweight on a good day no matter what he did to try and stay slim. Curtis had spent most of his youth lusting after men that were just looking for the next fuck with another hot guy.

He had tried and tried to be noticed at the bars. He had worn the newest fashions, had his hair done, even gotten his teeth bleached and a manicure, all to live the fantasy that he was one of them, one of the hot guys. Curtis had been exhausted trying to keep up with the crowd and finally realized that he had never been part of it in the first place.

He remembered when that had happened. He had been having a beer on the back patio, smoking a cigarette and talking to Sasha. They heard a guy close to them say, "Oh, look at the puppy, he thinks he's cute!"

His friend had laughed and said, "I'm surprised they had jeans in that size."

Sasha had turned on them and whipped a finger in their faces. "Curtis is twice the man that either of you are."

"You got that right, he's twice the size!" one of the men said, laughing.

Sasha had thrown her drink into his face. Not quite done, she grabbed Curtis's beer and dumped it over the other one. She let the plastic cups drop and hooked her arm through Curtis's. "Let's blow this pop stand, honey. Someone forgot to take out the trash."

Curtis had stopped trying to be like everyone else at that point. Instead he was just himself, and he was so much happier for it. He hadn't realized how miserable he had been. Sasha was thrilled. "It's about time you understood what an awesome guy you are. I would have snapped you up ages ago if you weren't queer as a three-dollar bill wrapped around a tangerine."

The memory made Curtis smile. His smile widened as he looked down at Devon. He was so peaceful when he slept, the dark lashes laying against his skin and his dark hair all ruffled up, his lips kissably supple. Curtis didn't think he had ever seen anything so beautiful.

Curtis watched as Devon's eyelids began to flutter and then Devon's gorgeous brown eyes were looking up at him. "Hello, lover," Devon said.

"Did I wake you?"

"Well I could feel your energy. It was really intense. It was interrupting the dream I was having."

"What was the dream?"

"I had you bent over your dining room table. You can fill in the blanks."

"Or we could do that later. I'll bet we put your dream to shame."

Sitting up, Devon grabbed his pack of cigarettes off the bedside table. Curtis gave him a look. "What?"

"You're going to smoke? Before coffee?"

"Then get your sexy ass into the kitchen and make me some," Devon said, laughing.

"Already done." Curtis reached over to his bedside table and handed Devon a mug of coffee. "It's black, just as you like it."

"You really are an angel, you know that?" Taking a grateful sip, Devon leaned forward to kiss Curtis softly on the lips. "Can I smoke now?"

"Yes, as long as you share."

Devon handed him a cigarette and then lit both of them. After taking a drag, Devon looked at him and asked, "So what were you thinking about?"

"Oh, nothing."

"The look on your face when I opened my eyes wasn't created by nothing. C'mon, babe, tell me. What's up?"

"You're going to think I'm silly."

"You are silly, it's one of your best qualities."

Curtis took a few sips of coffee and a drag off his cigarette to give himself strength. "Well, I was thinking of when I knew you before."

Devon was shocked. "We knew each other before?"

"No, we never met. But you got around. I saw you around the bars."

"Oh, my reputation doth proceed me."

"You could say that. I watched you from afar, wondering what you were like and if all the rumours were true."

"I hope the rumours were kind to me."

"They were, but not nearly complimentary enough."

"Then what's the problem?"

"It's nothing."

"No one thinks that intensely when it's nothing. Now are you going to tell me, or am I going to have to tickle it out of you?"

"It really is nothing anymore. I'm just astounded by how people change, that's all."

"What do you mean? You got even cuter than you were before?"

Curtis kissed Devon quickly and then reached for his coffee. "No, well yes, thank you for noticing. Really, I was thinking to how I was before and how you were before. I never thought that the two of us would get together. I used to watch you as you worked the bars and dream of being with you. I'm pretty sure all the men did."

"Why didn't you approach me?"

"Because I didn't have one hundred dollars for a 'good time.'"

"Ouch. Point taken."

"I didn't like myself very much then because I was trying to be what everyone else thought I should be. You didn't look like you were having fun because you were trying to please everyone else."

Devon was touched that Curtis knew him so well after such a short time. He was moved beyond words for a moment.

He could only look at Curtis, at the gorgeous flecks of green in his almost golden eyes. "You are beautiful, you know that?"

"Honey, I'm fabulous. It takes a lot of work to look this cheap."

Devon kissed him and tried to convey in the kiss how wonderful it was to have someone truly know him. If it took a few more kisses, well, that was the price he had to pay.

Chapter Seventy-Three

The drive back to their apartment was a quiet one.

Mike was oddly silent. He didn't look upset, just pensive. Nancy was all for letting him be alone with his thoughts, but the silence was killing him. "So, I think that went well," he stated.

"Yeah, I think Cordellia will take good care of him. She seemed so happy. I hope that rubs off on William."

Mike descended into silence again. They drove on for a bit before Nancy said, "Sweetie, pull in over there."

"At Good Neighbours?" Mike gave Nancy a look. "I thought you said that their food gave you heartburn."

"That may be so, but I need grease to sop up some of that booze."

"We only had the one glass."

"With how Cordellia pours, it's more like three. C'mon handsome, I'm buying."

They settled themselves and ordered food. Nancy waited until they had ordered coffee before stretching his hand across the table and taking Michael's. "So, you okay?"

"I'm fine."

"Honey, I know that look. That's the look that says, 'I'm a big man and I'm fine and nothing can get to me.' I've seen you wear that one a lot, like when William broke your heart all those months ago."

"I'm fine, really."

Nancy gave him a pointed stare. "Honey, I love you, but that doesn't stop me from bitch-slapping you across the table and into next week. You've watched William slide into a dark area. That's gotta do something to your psyche. You were quiet as all get out at Cordellia's. You seemed tense and uncomfortable. So spill, please?"

"I'm confused, really. I mean, William was a strong and confident man who I loved with all my heart. I thought he was the love of my life. Now he's this sad mess, desperate to find the happiness that he once had but threw away, needing to find what's left of himself to salvage some part of who he is."

"He's lost, babe. But we'll help him find his way back. He took a few wrong steps, that's all. It happens to all of us."

Their food came and they were silent for a moment, digging into eggs and bacon. Then Michael spoke again, "I still remember the first time I saw him. He was like the king of the bars, knowing just how to command a room. Everyone always watched him, but he wasn't conceited about it. He was so handsome. Is it wrong that I miss that man, the one that I was with for so long? How can I love someone like you but still have feeling for what used to be?"

"You never really got a chance to let go or heal after what William did to you. Plus, you're human. You would be a sorry individual if you weren't moved in some way by what David did to William. It's one of the reasons I love you."

"Then what do I do about it?"

"We've done all we can. We just have to let things play out how they will. William will be safe. Cordellia will look after him. We will, too. But you and I need to do something for you."

"What's that?"

"We need to have a letting go ceremony."

"Is this a thing?"

"It is. Do you still have the ring he gave you?"

Blushing slightly, Mike pulled out his old ring from his pocket. "I keep it with my change. I won't lose it that way."

"Well now, after breakfast, we're going to go somewhere and help you let go. Hold onto that ring for now, we're going to need it."

Chapter Seventy-Four

"I'm ready," said Dava.

Poppy looked up from her newspaper and smiled. "Ready for what? Another cup of coffee?"

They had gone out last night and Dava had gotten a little drunk. Poppy let her, as everyone needed to blow off some steam every now and again. Of course, she was the designated driver because she couldn't drink, but she was okay with that. It was just nice to see Dava letting lose. She had held herself in check for so long; Poppy couldn't imagine what it must have been like, to live life in fear. She would do everything in her power to make sure Dava didn't have to go through that again.

"No, I'm ready to take the next step, to take complete control of my life." Dava stood and walked over to Poppy, a brightness in her eyes. "I want to get married, I want to be completely free. At first, I thought it was enough to just leave him, but now I've realized that I need my whole life back. I also want to introduce you to my boys since you're going to be their new mom."

Poppy was momentarily silent. She was filled with so much emotion, all competing to get out at once. Finally, she stood and took Dava's hands. "Are you sure? This will be a battle. He won't let you go that easily."

Nodding, Dava said, "I'm sure. I've never been so certain. I want to build a life with you, to realize my dream. I don't want to be afraid anymore."

She let go to walk over to the small desk that Poppy kept in the corner of the living room. Dava took hold of a stack of papers. "I've already drawn up the papers. All I have to do is file for a simple divorce. It's been long enough."

"How did you do this?"

"Justin helped me. I downloaded the forms off of the internet. He helped me go through them and fill them out correctly so that I didn't miss anything. I even have the marriage certificate. I don't know why I held onto that for so long, but I always wondered if it would come in handy. Now it finally has."

"But doesn't he need to be served with the papers?"

"He does, but by a third party. Justin brought them to Fred last week. I wanted to wait until it was all done until I told you."

"You've kept this from me? I wanted to help you through it, to be there for you while you went through this."

"But you have been! Don't you see? I think this was something I had to do on my own, so that we could start our lives fresh."

"Never mind that Justin helped you."

"That's beside the point. I just wanted to surprise you and to make it up to you."

"What do you have to make up to me?"

"When I said no to your marriage proposal, I knew that hurt you, and there's nothing I can do to take that hurt away. I can't erase it, can't redo the moment. When all this is said and done, I hope you're going to be willing to propose again."

Tears welled in Poppy's eyes. She pulled Dava close to her and said, "Of course! But, I think maybe this time you should propose, seeing as I botched up the last one."

Dava let out a bark of laughter just as there was a loud knock at the door. There was another knock, almost like a boom of thunder. It made a deep chill run through Poppy and she clutched Dava tightly.

"Were you expecting anyone?"

"No, you?"

"I don't think so. All the boys have keys anyway."

"Maybe a next-door neighbour?" Dava asked.

"They would ring the bell."

After another thundering boom, the door shook on its hinges. "I'd say whoever they are, they want to get in very badly. Don't open the door, honey."

"I'm not going to." Poppy grabbed her phone and dialed 911. The dispatcher picked up right away.

"911, what is the nature of your emergency?"

"There is an intruder trying to break into my home."

There was another earth-shattering boom and the door shook even further. A voice called out, "Come let me in, Dava! You think you can just divorce me? You think you can just cast me away? You otta know I'll have something to say!"

"Please help, please come as soon as you can."

"Someone will be there momentarily, there are police in the area, please stay on the line so we—"

The front door flew open and slammed against the wall. Fred was standing there in his wife beater and jeans, and there was a menacing look in his eyes. Poppy put the phone down on the table and hoped that he didn't see it or think she had done something stupid.

He lumbered into the living room and slammed the door behind him. Then his eyes fell on Dava and went wild. Poppy could smell the booze off of him from where she was, and from the look on his face knew that his next movement would cause pain.

"Did you think I'd just stand aside and let you do this to me? You've already taken my boys, you think I would let you remove yourself out of my life?"

He punched Dava hard in the face and she nearly went down. Poppy heard the crack of his knuckles on the bones of her face and that sound spurred her into action. She ran towards them and put herself in between them, knowing that she had to keep Dava safe.

"You leave her alone, you fucking asshole!" Poppy screamed.

"If it isn't the new pussy! One pussy wasn't good enough for Dava was it? She had to snatch your snatch, too! Fucking cunt." He slapped her and then punched her in the stomach. Poppy experienced a hot, fierce pain in her stomach that ran up her body and she could only think, The baby—he's hurt the baby!

Fred punched her again and then Poppy was down on the ground. She curled herself into a ball even as Fred drew back his foot and kicked her in the stomach once, twice, three times. The baby, Poppy thought. The baby.

There was the sound of breaking glass and then Poppy knew nothing but darkness. She struggled to stay awake and alert—What happened to Dava?—but the pull of the darkness was too strong and Poppy finally let it have her.

Chapter Seventy-Five

"Now that everyone else has gone, let's you and I have a little chat."

William looked warily at Cordellia. Blaine and Nancy had left. He hadn't been alone with Cordellia in months, not since the whole thing with David had started and he had lost himself along the way. "Okay."

"There's no need to be nervous. You might have been an asshole recently, but you're still one of my boys. And can you tell me when one of them hasn't been an asshole? William, it's the human condition to be one every now and again." She held out her hand. "Come with me."

"Where are we going?"

"Out to the garden. I like to sit out there when it's sunny, so I can drink while in the nude in peace without the neighbours looking at me." She let out a laugh as her eyes sparkled. "Just kidding, I thought it would be nice to be outside and have the sun shine down on us for a bit."

Taking her hand, William stood, and they went out into the back garden. On the way there, he noticed a ring on the third finger of her left hand. Turning in so that he could stare at the ring, William brought her hand closer to his face. The diamond was almost blinding.

"When did this happen?" William whispered.

"Last night."

"Why didn't you say anything? Does Blaine know? He's going to go nuts for you."

"Well, we had a bit to be getting on with, didn't we?" Cordellia gave William's cheek a soft pat. "It's all good, I'll tell everyone when I see them next. Right now, though, let's go and talk amongst ourselves, shall we?"

"Are you happy, Cordellia?"

"Deliriously so. I don't know that I deserve so much happiness, but I'll take it while it's here."

"You deserve all the happiness in the world."

"So do you, child, so do you."

William let out a huff and marched quickly towards a bench. "No, I don't. I've fucked everything up. I'm fucked up."

Cordellia sat down beside him and took one of his hands in her own. "William, we're all fucked up. Human beings as a theory are a really wonderful idea. In practice? Less so. Have you ever noticed that we create our own drama? Just when we think we have everything, we do something stupid to throw all that perfection in the trash."

"You don't do that."

"No, dear. I don't, but I've learned from my mistakes. You're young. You have so many mistakes to make yet and so much time to do them in—you're a babe in the woods."

"I'm not a chicken, I'm twenty-eight."

"A mere puppy, I believe that's the other term you use? Why are you so desperate to seek perfection so early on? I'm in my sixties and am far from perfect. Perfection is overrated, my dear boy."

William had tried to hold them back, but the tears came anyway. They slid down, leaving tracks across his cheeks as if they were made of glass. "I've fucked everything up, Cordellia. I've lost everything."

"No, you haven't, William. You have the boys and you have me. That's something, isn't it?"

She pulled him closer to her and he put his head on her shoulder. Cordellia held him as he cried, the tears soaking into her dress, hot and urgent. She rubbed his back and whispered to him that it would be okay.

Cordellia only hoped it was true.

Chapter Seventy-Six

Chuck hadn't spoken to Sebastian since last night.

He hadn't known what to say. Still didn't know. Cassandra had stood there as bold as brass and said that she was Sebastian's daughter and that Sebastian was his mother. He shook his head. Chuck could barely look at him, and they were living together. Yes, this is a good way to start off a living arrangement, with lies and deceit. Isn't that what everyone does?

There was a knock on the bedroom door. Cassandra had made a home in the second bedroom, and Sebastian had slept on the couch. Chuck had been too upset last night from coming home to finding Cassandra. When Sebastian had confirmed she was his daughter, Chuck had hidden away, not trusting himself to speak. He still wasn't sure what to say.

He knew it was Sebastian on the other side of the door. He spread his right hand flat against the door and wondered if Sebastian was doing the same thing. It would be romantic if it wasn't so fucked up.

There was another soft knock at the door and then Chuck heard Sebastian's voice. "Chuck? Charles? Can we talk?"

"We're talking just fine now."

"I don't want to talk to you through a piece of wood. Can you please open the door?"

Chuck took in a deep breath and slowly opened the door. Standing there, looking haggard, was Sebastian. Chuck was surprised by the surge of love he felt for him, even after all of this. Sebastian looked as if he had been beat up. Chuck wondered vaguely if the couch was that uncomfortable or if Sebastian felt battered on the inside.

"I'm sorry," he said. "I'm so sorry."

"Before you start apologizing, how about you tell me what the fuck happened? I suppose the calls you've been trying to dodge have been Cassandra's?"

"Yes, and her father. He was the one calling me in the beginning. Then Cassandra started calling."

"So, do you want to start there? Why would you not talk to your ex?"

"Because he was from a different part of my life. I cut ties with him and my daughter when I chose to become who I really was."

"You left your daughter behind? That's really cold."

"I know, and I didn't say I was proud of it."

"Surely it would have been okay having a daughter. I mean, there are kids with two gay dads now and everything."

"It was Kyle…" Sebastian took another deep breath. "He just couldn't deal with it. He kept asking me to reconsider, to really think things through. I told him again and again and again that I had thought things though, that I was done thinking and was going to do what I needed to do to be happy."

"I take it that didn't make him happy."

"No, it didn't. He said I had blindsided him, but I told him I was done blindsiding myself."

"What do you mean?"

"I had spent so long lying to myself about who I was. I knew my body was wrong, that I wasn't a woman, I was a man. I lied to myself and married Kyle. When I got pregnant, I figured that having a baby would make me feel more like a woman."

"Did it?"

Sebastian nodded. "It did for a bit. How can you not feel like a woman carrying a child around inside of you? But after a few years, the urges came back. The urge to really live my life the way it was supposed to be. I talked to Kyle and he said that he wouldn't be in a relationship with a man, that he wasn't a freak like me."

Chuck snorted. "Thinks a lot of us, doesn't he?"

"No, it's not that he's homophobic. He just didn't understand the whole trans thing, having a true self that needed desperately to come out. That was too much for him and I understood that."

"When did you decide to leave?"

"When Cassandra was eleven. I figured she was old enough for Kyle could raise her on his own. I left and filed for divorce the next day. I knew that my marriage was over, that I could no longer exist as the woman I was. I could only be the man I was destined to be."

"But why cut your daughter out of your life?"

Sebastian sighed. It was a deep sigh, full of sadness. "It was easier that way. A clean break from everything in my past and a new beginning for my future. I went through the steps I needed to do for my surgeries, therapy, all of that. It was a long hard road. Then, five years ago, I finally felt I was the man I was meant to be."

"Still though, cutting off your daughter...I don't know if I could have done that."

"It was the one regret I've lived with for so long. It's kind of like a gift having her here, if you know what I mean. The very fact that she still wants to see me is like the greatest gift. I know you didn't sign up for this, for being a father to a twenty-one-year-old. I understand if you want to call it quits and find someone else. I'll understand, but I won't like it."

Standing, Chuck turned to look at Sebastian with a stern look in his eyes. "Now you listen here, mister. And you listen good. Are your ears open?"

Sebastian nodded. "Yes."

"Good, 'cause I'm only going to say this once. I love you."

"That's it? You tell me you love me all the time."

"I wasn't done. I'll start again. I love you. We are starting our new life together, building a home together. Something I never thought would happen or thought I would want so desperately. Do you think I'm just going to walk away after something like this? You're the only man that I've ever really loved. You and I are together now, forever and a day if you'll have me. I'm not going away over this. Okay?"

There were tears in Sebastian's eyes. "Okay."

"Now, if you try to keep something like this from me again, we're going to have serious words and I'll have to kick your ass from here to Sunday of next month. People who love each other don't keep secrets. They tell each other what's going on and what's happening when it's happening, okay?"

"Okay," Sebastian said softly.

"I'm going to kiss you now," Chuck said.

Sebastian stood and held Chuck close before touching his lips to Chuck's. The fire ran though Chuck, and he thought he had never wanted someone else more than this. Chuck deepened the kiss, and his body was responding in all the ways it should when there was a knock at the door.

"Are you guys finished gaying out?" Cassandra asked, followed by, "What's for breakfast?"

Chapter Seventy-Seven

Everything was going right in the world, Blaine thought.

They were helping William, trying to stick it to David, and he was getting married. He had never thought of getting married; he had never met anyone he pictured spending his life with. Blaine had been too afraid after David to trust someone that deeply.

Blaine had been with a lot of different men, but none of them had touched his heart this way. There had always been something just under the surface that he couldn't get to, that they wouldn't let him see.

Then, there was David. He had taken more from him than any other man. David had left him broken and he had stayed because he thought there was hope, that he was making headway. However, every single time, he had been wrong. David had not loved him. He had merely looked at Blaine as some sort of possession, a thing to be played with and taught its place.

It had taken Blaine months to get over David, even though Blaine knew David was a bad man and there was nothing good in him. He had thought about it and wondered if he had loved what could have been, rather than the man himself.

It didn't matter; he was free of him even if William wasn't. He had to help William as much as he could, but Blaine knew that William had to want to help himself. He was taking steps to do that and hopefully would succeed. Blaine knew firsthand how difficult that was.

Feeling lighter than he had in a long time, he let himself into the apartment he now shared with Justin and found him waiting in the foyer. "What's wrong?" Blaine asked.

"Why, does it seem like something's wrong?"

"Well, you only look like this if shit has really hit the fan." Blaine inspected Justin's face and saw the hard lines drawn upon it. "Judging from your expression, I'd say something really awful happened."

"How do I look exactly?"

"Like you're constipated, nauseated, have a migraine, and you're about to throw up."

Justin gave him a confused stare. "You've never seen me like that."

"I have when you're trying to fill out a crossword. Seriously, what's wrong? Are you okay?"

"Well, we'll have to see. I have something to tell you." Justin wrung his hands.

"What is it, babe?" Blaine went to him and took Justin's hands in his. "You know that you can tell me anything."

"I know, I know that, but this is big. This is the biggest thing you can do for me right now. I will love you forever and I will be your love slave."

There was the sound of footsteps coming down the hallway.

"And I'm going to take this moment to say that I'm sorry."

"Justin, what are you sorry for?"

What Justin was sorry for became apparent a moment later when Victoria stood in the doorway to the foyer. She glanced at Blaine with inquisitive eyes. "Oh, Justin dear. I'm out of tea. Your friend is home, perhaps he can make me a cup? Why are you both whispering out here? I have to organize my room if I'm going to stay in this place. This apartment is barley habitable!"

She clicked back down the hallway and Blaine glared at Justin.

"I love you?" Justin said meekly.

Chapter Seventy-Eight

"So, what exactly are we doing out here?" Michael asked.

"What we talked about before. We're going to let all your hurt go."

"In the backyard?"

"Yes," Nancy said, giving Michael a grin. "It's a perfectly fine place."

"It doesn't seem very mystical for a letting go ceremony."

"Any place is a good place for letting go. Do you have his ring?"

They were standing out in the backyard in front of the old oak tree. It had been there when Nancy had moved in to the small house and over the years he had watched it grow. He always came out to sit underneath it when he wanted a moment of quiet, a spot to think and work through stuff that made his head too full. He had spent so much time here after Devon.

Michael took it out of his pocket. "Right here."

"Good. Now hold it in the palm of your hand."

"Which one?"

"Your right one. Left is for taking in, right is for letting go."

"How do you know this shit?"

"It's not shit, and I've been around. You get to know stuff that way."

Michael put the ring in his right hand and closed the ring up inside his fist. "Okay, now what?"

"Now we say a few words. I'll go first."

"Are we, like, praying?"

"No, just sending out our intentions to the world. Don't

look at me that way, Mike, people have been doing stuff like this for thousands of years. Have an open mind, for fuck's sake."

"I do have an open mind. I'm with you, aren't I?"

"Ouch, remind me to smack you later. I'll go first just to show you how it's done."

Nancy took a deep breath and closed his eyes for a few seconds. When he opened them, he cupped Michael's right hand in his left and looked down at the ring.

"Thank you, William. Thank you for showing Michael a valuable lesson. Thank you for teaching him what he was worth to you so that he could grow beyond that. Thank you for loving him in your way to show him that he deserved more."

Nancy remained silent for a bit, the only sound was the early morning breeze. Then Nancy turned to Michael and said, "Your turn."

"I think you did well enough for both of us."

"Michael. I'm not doing this for me. I'm doing this for you. You have to say something because it's you who's letting go. Take a moment to think about it, then say what comes to mind."

Michael nodded, feeling a little silly. He took a deep breath and said: "William. Thank you for the love you showed me. Thank you for showing me what I didn't want in a partner or a husband. Thank you for showing me that I was stronger than you, that I mattered more to myself, that my happiness mattered more than staying in an unhappy relationship. Thank you for showing me that true love is not something you say, it's something you do. I hope you find your release. Thank you."

Nancy looked at him with a watery smile. "That was lovely."

"What do we do now?" Michael's voice was soft when he spoke.

"Now we bury the ring in the earth. And then you will be free."

Michael and Nancy both bent down to dig a small hole in the soil on the ground in front of the tree with their hands. Michael placed the ring inside the hole and Nancy covered it back up and patted the mound of dirt down.

They stood, and Michael drew Nancy into a hug and kissed him deeply. When Nancy pulled back, he said, "What was that for?"

"For loving me." Michael kissed him again, just as deeply. "And that was for letting me love you."

They stood there, holding each other, and listened to the rustle of leaves in the breeze.

Chapter Seventy-Nine

Romilda didn't trust happiness.

It faded far too quickly, was gone in an instant like a really good bottle of wine. Happiness was best left as a memory, of a beautiful summer day that changed quickly when the storm came.

However, looking at Cordellia, Romilda had to admit that maybe this happiness thing wasn't so bad. She had never seen Cordellia looking so young. She had a glow to her cheeks and the clouds were gone from her eyes as if they had been lifted. It was as if there were no storms inside of her anymore.

"Well, look at you! You're positively glowing!"

Cordellia blushed. "I must be. Joe asked me to marry him!" Cordellia let out a laugh seeing the shocked expression on Romilda's face. "Gosh, you could be happy for me!"

"I am happy, Cordy, it's just so sudden!"

"I've waited forever for this. At least it feels like that."

"Didn't you just meet up with him again? Why the rush?"

"We've waited our whole lives for each other, so that's hardly a rush."

"Well, why now?"

"Why not now?" Cordellia looked at Romilda and frowned. "That's it, you look like you need to take your medicine."

She got up from her kitchen table and picked out two glasses. "What do you want? Wine, scotch, vodka, gin? Oh, I have some lovely Grand Marnier. We could have that."

"You know, I'd love a nice cup of tea. Herbal if you have it."

Cordellia pulled a face. "Tea? Oh dear, it must be serious."

She put the glasses away and took out two heavy mugs and put the kettle on to boil. "Now, will you tell me what's going on? What has you so down?"

"That's just it. I'm not down. It's going beautifully with Gaston. He's wonderful, he's okay with me being trans. I mean, he knows, Cordy, he knows and he's okay with it. He told me that he was in love with me!"

Cordellia let out a loud cheer of joy. "Oh Romy! That calls for booze, fuck the tea, we can have that any old time. So, how is he in the sack?"

"He's lovely and wonderful. He's attentive and sensitive and funny as all get out. Gaston is intelligent, and he loves me. Cordellia, he actually loves me and knows everything about me."

"Then why are you acting like this is the end of the world?"

"Because! What if I fuck it up? What if it all crashes down around me like a house of cards? What if I screw everything up?"

"Do you love him?" Cordellia asked this quietly, the two wine glasses back in her hand.

"God, yes!"

"Have you told him?"

"No, I haven't."

"Why not?"

"Because, I'm afraid the dream will end when I do. I'm afraid that when he has my love he'll cast it away."

Cordellia poured wine into the glasses and brought them to the table. She put them down and sat across from Romilda again, taking one of Romilda's hands in one of her own. "That's part of what love is like. It's a journey, Romy, but you have to be willing to start it. Here."

She held up her glass and Romilda did the same.

"To taking that first step," Cordellia said.

They clinked glasses and Romilda wondered if that's what the music of stars sounded like.

Chapter Eighty

"Absolutely not," Blaine said.

Justin almost pouted. "What do you want me to do? She's my mother."

"She's a horrible person. I will not have her under this roof." He almost hissed the words.

"But she's my mother! Would you have me kick my mother out of the house? She just left my father. Would you kick Cordelia out of the house if she needed our help?"

"No, but she's not an absolute bitch."

"Look, I know she can be difficult—"

"Difficult isn't the word. She treats you horribly and in case you haven't noticed, she's none too fond of me, either. We can't let her stay here."

"Babe, she's my mother."

"Okay, then I don't want her to stay here."

They heard the clicking of high heeled shoes on the hardwood again and Victoria was standing in the doorway to the rest of the apartment. "I take it that I'm the one who has inspired this hissing conversation? Whisper or not, your walls are very thin. I've heard every word. You two, come with me. I hope you don't mind, but I've poured us all a stiff drink. Lord knows I need one and by the looks of the colour of your skin, Blaine, you do, too."

She clicked out again and Blaine and Justin shared an open-mouthed look of shock. Blaine let out a long breath. "Wow, she's got the mom look down pat."

They both followed her into the living room where she was sitting in front of the coffee table with three glasses of wine in front of her. "Drink up, gentlemen. The wine doesn't wait for anyone."

They each took a glass and Victoria held up hers. "Cheers."

"To what?" Blaine asked.

She turned her gaze upon him and, unless he was much mistaken, gave him a small smile. "To life. To love. To a good home."

They all clinked glasses together and drank. Justin was so nervous he had drained half of his glass already. Seeing this, Victoria tutted. "Are you an animal, Justin?"

"No, Mother."

"Good, because only animals slurp their wine. Trust me, I know. Your father could down a glass in one go. Such a waste of good wine."

"Mother, what happened?"

"Oh, nothing major, I just caught your father having yet another affair with his newest secretary. It's his thirtieth or fortieth one. I've had enough, son, I really have. I'm not getting any younger, and I have to live my life. Do you know what I mean, son?"

Justin gave Blaine a loving look. "Yes, Mom, I do."

"So," Victoria looked at Blaine again. "You're the man who's stolen my son's heart."

"I can't steal what was freely given."

"True. I assume that you gave him yours in return?"

"Yes, ma'am, I did."

"Oh, a boy with manners! How delightful. But no ma'am's, please. That makes me feel old. Victoria will do fine, or Mom when you feel up to it, seeing as you're getting married. Now," she motioned at the art around the apartment, "Justin tells me these are yours? You have a fine hand with a brush, Blaine. What galleries have you shown your work at?"

"None, I just do this for fun."

"Oh, that simply won't do. Your art must be seen! Drink your wine boys, I'm going to go make a few phone calls. I know quite a few people that run their own galleries. In the meantime, let's think about dinner, shall we? I would love some gorgeous Thai food. Your father hated Thai food, and I haven't had it in years."

She dug her cell phone out of a pocket and, taking her glass of wine, left the room. Justin let out another long breath.

"She's kind of like a train, isn't she? You don't see her coming," Blaine stated.

"You don't know the half of it." Justin sighed.

Blaine moved closer to Justin and took his wine glass and put both of theirs down on the coffee table. "If your mother stays, it's because I love you. You know that, right?"

"I do. Indeed I do."

"And if she gets bitchy or loses it with us, she's gone. You hear that? If she causes any drama, she's done."

"Understandable."

"And if she pushes you around, I have the right to kick her ass…at least metaphorically. Are we clear?"

"Like crystal."

"Good. I love you." Blaine leaned in closer and kissed Justin softly on the lips.

"And I love you. So much."

"I know, it helps that I'm fabulous, doesn't it?"

"I'll admit that does help quite a bit."

Blaine's cell phone rang, and he looked down at the caller display. It read "City View Hospital." Knowing that this couldn't be good, he had thoughts of Cordellia run through his head, Blaine clicked on the answer button. "Hello?"

Chapter Eighty-One

"Hello, is this Blaine Andrews?" The voice was soft and matronly. The voice you hear from your mother before she doles out bad news.

"Yes, this is Blaine Andrews. Who's calling please?"

"This is Cindy Johnson, I'm a nurse at the City View Hospital. Poppy McBride was brought in to the hospital an hour ago with serious injuries and your number was marked as in case of emergency on her phone contact list."

"Poppy? What's wrong? Is she okay? No, of course she's not. Can I come see her?"

"Are you family?" Cindy asked. "She's still in observation, but only family will be allowed to visit her in intensive care."

"Both of her parents have passed on and she was an only child. I'm all the family she has."

He heard Cindy take in a breath and let it out slowly. "I guess in this case we can make an exception. If you come now, you can find me at the emergency desk."

"Thank you, we'll be right there." Blaine took in his own deep breath. "How is the baby? Is the baby alright? What happened?"

"It's probably best if you come in. I can tell you more here."

"But is the baby alright?"

"Please, I won't discuss this over the phone. Surely you understand that."

"Okay, okay, thank you. We'll be right in."

Blaine hung up the phone and looked at Justin. Justin was looking back at him with wide eyes.

"Poppy? What's wrong with Poppy?" Justin asked

urgently.

"They won't tell me over the phone, so I know as much as you do. We have to go now."

"Of course. Let me get my wallet and keys and we can go."

"Go?" Victoria had come back into the living room. "Where do you think you're going? Blaine, I have the most marvelous news!"

"It'll have to wait ma'am. A friend of mine has been hurt. Justin and I have to go to the hospital."

"But Justin!" She turned to her son. "I just got here! You can't abandon me in my hour of need."

"Oh, for God's sake, Mother, every hour is your hour of need!"

"Justin this is serious! I'm in serious trouble!"

Striding over to his mother, Blaine watched as Justin tried to control himself, as he tried to keep his emotions in check. It didn't work.

"Can you think of anyone but yourself for just one minute? One fucking minute, Mother! A friend of mine, the woman that is having my baby, is hurt and in trouble. She's at the hospital and that's where we're going. You can come with us or stay here, it doesn't matter either way to me."

"What? A woman is having your what?"

"Come or go, mother. Choose."

"I'll come of course! I can't wait to meet the woman that is having my grandchild!"

Chapter Eighty-Two

Waiting for Dylan to arrive, Rebecca could hardly contain her excitement. When she saw him walking up to her building, she didn't give him a chance to buzz up but instead ran down to meet him at the front door.

She felt like a schoolgirl, her heart too big in her chest, as if it was unable to contain everything she was feeling. Running to him, she threw her arms around him and kissed him, trying to communicate everything she still couldn't say. Loving someone was a dangerous business, but she was a warrior.

Dylan kissed her back, deepening the kiss. Finally, when they broke apart, she saw that his eyes had gone wide and his skin was flushed. Rebecca ran a hand over his chest and felt his heart beating hard as if he had run a mile.

"What brought that on?" he asked her.

"Nothing…everything."

"Okay, that clears things up."

She laughed and realized once again that she hadn't truly laughed in a long, long time. "No, sorry. I meant to keep this from you for a little while longer while I worked out how to say it to you. I'm not good with words, Dylan. Shopping is my creative outlet."

"Just speak from the heart. My heart is listening."

"Gods, Dylan, if I tell you what I'm feeling in here"—she touched spot on her chest where her heart lay beneath—"and you don't feel the same way, I think I'm going to die. Of embarrassment, rather than a fatal wound, but still."

Dylan grinned at her. "I hope you don't die. I still have to take you dancing somewhere in the moonlight." He took her hands. "It's all good, Rebecca. We have time. Let's take the time to get to know each other, okay?"

She reached out and touched his chest. "But I want to tell you."

"There's no need. I feel the same way. I mean, you're the only woman I've gone on a marathon shopping trip with and lived to tell the tale. You're gorgeous and funny and smart to boot. Plus, I love spending time with you. What's not to like?"

The word "like" stung a bit, but Rebecca didn't want to read too much into it. "Oh, yeah, well…I am pretty fabulous."

"Cool, let's go get something to eat. I'm starving."

He took her hand in his and led her around the corner from her apartment building. She blinked back the tears. She had been all ready to tell Dylan that she loved him. She had never told any guy that.

Sure, she loved her parents, her family, and said it to them all the time. But never a man. And here she was, on the verge of telling Dylan, and he didn't want to hear it.

"Hold on a second, I have to get something from my car."

She nodded and watched as he reached into the back seat. When he turned, he was holding a dozen long stemmed roses. Her heart beat faster as he walked towards her with a smile on his face.

"What are those for?" Rebecca asked, trying not to sound breathless but not succeeding very well.

"They're for you. A man should always give a woman flowers, especially when he tells her that he loves her."

Her whole world went still. "What did you say?"

Dylan held out the flowers to her. "I love you, Rebecca. Have since the night we met. I think I've dreamed of you for years now but didn't know it was you I saw in my dreams. I don't know where we're going or where we're headed, but I want to go there with you."

She accepted the flowers and stared into his eyes. And then hit him with the flowers.

"You complete asshole," she said. "I was going to tell you first and you took that away from me."

"What? Shouldn't it be the man who says it first?"

"It doesn't fucking matter who says it first. The thing is, I wanted to be first." She hit him softly with the flowers again for good measure.

"Does that mean you love me?"

"Yes, you fucker. I love you." She stalked towards the car.

"I thought we were going for brunch?"

"We're going shopping first, then you're going to take me out for a fancy breakfast."

"What do you need to get now?"

"It's what you're going to get me. I need a really fancy purse and Coach is having a sale."

"The flowers look rather damaged."

"Oh, you're going to buy me a new dozen of those, too. C'mon, hot stuff, times a wasting."

Chapter Eighty-Three

"Have you been able to reach everyone?" Blaine asked.

They were driving as fast as the law allowed. Blaine didn't know what he would find at the hospital and what state Poppy was in, but he was determined to be there for her. Justin felt the same way; it was his kid, after all.

"I've gotten hold of everyone. Chuck and Sebastian, Mike and Nancy, Cordellia and Romilda. They're all going to meet us there. I figure since you're the contact though, they'll let you in first."

"And you," Blaine said. "You're the father of her unborn child. They have to let you in."

"So, explain to me how you ended up getting a girl pregnant, Justin," Victoria said from the back seat. "I'm really curious as to how that happened. Not that I'm not happy of course, a grandchild is a grandchild, but I thought you preferred…people like Blaine, not ladies."

"Now is so not the time, Mother."

"Well, I have a right to know, don't I? How can you expect me to welcome the child into the family without knowing how it came to be?"

"That'll have to wait, Mother, really. I will tell you, but now is not the time." He turned left, and the City View Hospital came into view.

"But I have a right to know!" Victoria said.

Justin sped into a parking space and shut off the car. He turned to look at his mother. "No, you don't. You don't have a right to know. You haven't been part of my life for a long time and now you want in when I've given you what you want?" Justin snorted. "Right. You have a lot more making up to do before I let you in again, Victoria. You have no idea."

Victoria looked as if she had been slapped. "You've never called me by my first name before."

"I've never had to before. But you're just not listening. There are things more important in my life than what you want or what you need. It's time you started taking note of them." He opened his car door. "Now you can stay in the car or you can come with us, but you won't speak until spoken to, understand?"

"I will not stay in the car like a child!" Victoria spat.

"Then stop acting like one," Justin shot back.

Blaine and Justin got out of the car and waited for Victoria to exit the vehicle. Blaine turned to him. "You were a little harsh with her."

"She deserves it."

"Maybe she does, but now isn't the time, babe. We have to focus on Poppy." Blaine took hold of Justin's hands and held them. "We have to make sure Poppy and Dava are all right."

Justin looked at Blaine with tears in his eyes. One tear fell and ran along his cheek. "What if something terrible has happened to them?"

"We'll get through it, together. Okay?"

"Okay."

They kissed softly, trying to give each other strength. Standing some ways from them, Victoria watched them and wiped a tear from her eye before it fell.

Chapter Eighty-Four

"I can't wait for you to meet her," Curtis said.

They had lazed around in Devon's apartment for most of the morning when Curtis's cell phone rang. He answered it and was soon gushing about him. It made Devon blush. As much as he loved being a hot lay, hearing someone describe him to someone else always made him feel uncomfortable. Devon felt obligated to live up to the picture the other person painted of him.

The person who Curtis was currently gushing to was his best friend Sasha. Devon didn't do well with friends; Nancy had proved that. Though, to be fair, his treatment of Nancy probably had a lot to do with that.

Still, Devon had to admit he was nervous. I mean, this was someone Curtis loved like a sister. Would she like him or hate him on sight? He pulled his hand away from Curtis's and wiped the sweat off on his pants.

"What's wrong?" Curtis asked.

"Just nervous."

"You, nervous? Mr. Joe Cool?"

"Hey, I can get nervous."

"I've never seen you like this before. You would be approached by random men all the time to do the nasty with them, and you never broke a sweat."

"I've never met a friend of someone I cared about before."

"What about Nancy?" Curtis asked, taking Devon's hand back. "You must have met his friends."

"I did, but I was Mr. Cool then, right? I loved him, but I wasn't in love with him if that makes sense."

"It does. You wore a lot of armour back then. It's a wonder

anyone was able to break through it."

They were walking towards the East Town mall. Cars were moving along the street and people were milling around them. It sounded like music to Devon. "Nancy tried, he really did, and he was close but not close enough."

"So, you liked him enough to sleep with him, but aside from that…?"

"Yeah, that's pretty much it. I only realized that I was in love with him afterwards. By then, it was too late."

"So, what is it about me that broke past your wall?"

"I don't really have any walls anymore."

"P'shaw. Everyone has walls. Yours are just a bit thinner now, that's all."

Devon stopped walking and pulled Curtis in for a kiss. It was slow and soft and warmed Devon down to his toes. "I could fall in love with you, Curtis," he said softly and waited with anticipation to hear what Curtis's reply would be.

He was quiet for a moment and Devon feared the worst until Curtis broke out into a grin that went from ear to ear. "I should damn well hope so. I'm one hot ticket, after all, and just too darn sexy for most people."

Letting out a laugh, Devon kissed him again. "Can't we go home and make out?"

"Honey, we did that yesterday and the day before, plus more. Besides, you can't keep me chained to your bed all the time, you know." Curtis gave Devon's hand a squeeze. "Relax, you'll like her."

They crossed the road and entered the shopping centre. The coffee shop, Spilled Beans, was right across from them. Sasha sat at one of the tables. On seeing Curtis, she stood and waved, smiling. They walked over, and Sasha gave Curtis a big hug.

"Babe! You're so thin! You've lost weight!" Sasha squealed.

"Well, beautiful, sex is good for your health!"

"How do you think I stay so healthy?"

"Sucking cock in public bathrooms?"

"Oh, no honey, don't you remember? That was your last job!"

They both lost it in a fit of giggling and Devon couldn't help but smile. He had never laughed with someone like that. He wanted to do that with Curtis. How times change, he thought. He was actually picturing a future with Curtis. A far cry from last year when all he could think of was his next fuck.

Curtis and Sasha stopped laughing and Curtis turned to him with a big smile. "Sasha, this is Devon." Curtis came closer and ran a hand along Devon's chest. Devon felt love blooming for Curtis then. He knew that Curtis was trying to calm him down.

Devon turned with a smile to Sasha and held out his hand. "Nice to meet you."

"Nice to meet you, too. I hear you used to be a whore. Have any diseases that Curtis should know about?"

Chapter Eighty-Five

When they entered the emergency room, the first thing Blaine saw were two police officers talking to the on-duty nurse. He approached the desk with growing caution, a knot of dread filling his stomach; he felt as if he were filled with lead. Victoria followed closely behind.

He held on so tightly to Justin's hand that Blaine could feel Justin's heartbeat thrumming through his skin. The nurse looked up when he cleared his throat. "Hello there. I'm Blaine Andrews. You called me about Poppy McBride? Is she okay?"

The nurse smiled thinly and then the smile turned into a frown. "I'm sorry Mr. Andrews. She's experienced a lot of trauma and has multiple lacerations to her face and body. She's in stable condition though."

"St-stable? That makes it sound as if her life is in danger."

"It was. But we've got everything under control. We're doing everything we can to make sure that she's comfortable."

"What about her baby?" Justin asked. Though the words were a whisper, everyone could hear them. Blaine loosened the grip he had on Justin's hand.

The nurse grimaced and put the small smile back on her face. "Who are you, sir?"

"I'm Justin Callaway. I'm the baby's father. I want to know if the baby is all right."

"You can see Poppy and Dava in a moment, but these officers would like to speak to you briefly first. Then I'll take you through."

"Dear God, Dava too?" Blaine said. He couldn't keep the volume of his voice down so that the words came out as a shout. "What happened?"

One of the officers, a gentleman with kind eyes and dark curling hair, took Blaine by the elbow. "Sir, we'd like to talk to you, just for a moment, and then you can go and see your friends."

"I'll wait here," Justin said.

"No sir, you better come with us. You said your name is Justin Callaway?"

"Yes."

"Then we need to speak with you as well."

Justin turned to Victoria and said, "Will you wait here?"

"Of course," she said. She placed a hand on his cheek. "Of course I will, son"

The nurse showed Blaine and Justin and the officers into a private room, normally a doctor's examination room. When the officer closed the door, the silence was deafening. Blaine turned to the officers and said, "Now can you tell me what happened?"

"First, we're very sorry you have to go through any of this. I'm Officer Daniels and this is Officer Johnson." A petite female officer with black hair, light brown skin, and severe cheek bones shook their hands. "Now, Mr. Callaway, you're a lawyer, correct?"

Justin looked flustered. "Yes, but how did you know that?"

"Because of this." Daniels pulled a piece of paper out of his pocket and unfolded it. It was the peace bond that he had drawn up for Dava.

"What does that have to do with anything?" Justin asked.

"It seems to have been the spark for what took place this evening." Officer Johnson said softly.

"What happened?!" Blaine didn't care that he was shouting, that he was losing his temper. The woman who was his sister of the heart was somewhere in this hospital and his only desire was to see her and make sure that she was okay.

The two officers exchanged a look and Officer Daniels spoke, his voice soft and low. Blaine wondered if they talked to everyone like that to keep them calm, or if it was just his natural way of speaking.

"Earlier this evening, Fred Jackson received this peace bond and divorce papers that had been filled out and filed."

"I know," Justin said. "I was the one that gave them to him."

"Well, your intentions were good, but Mr. Jackson paid Dava a visit. Poppy was with her. When Mr. Jackson broke the door down, Ms. McBride was able to dial 911. The phone dropped when Mr. Jackson attacked Ms. McBride but the dispatcher heard everything. We were the officers on scene and we arrested Mr. Jackson."

"What happened to Poppy and Dava?" Blaine whispered. He almost didn't want to know.

"By the time we got there, Poppy was on the ground and Dava was standing over Mr. Jackson with a fire poker. She sustained lacerations to her face and hands and bruising to her neck where Mr. Jackson choked her. He also broke her nose when he first struck her and further lacerations where she was cut when he threw her onto a glass table."

"And Poppy…?"

Officer Johnson spoke, in an even softer voice than before. Blaine didn't know if it was out of concern over Poppy or what she was about to tell them. "Ms. McBride suffered great trauma and bruising to her abdomen. Mr. Jackson punched her there several times and then kicked her repeatedly in the stomach when Ms. McBride went down. She's suffered internal bleeding…"

"And the baby?" Justin almost hissed these words.

Officer Johnson shook her head, "I'm sorry, Mr. Callaway."

Tears started sliding out of his eyes. Blaine hadn't even realized he was crying until he felt the tears there, but he did not reach up to wipe them away. "Can we see her now?" How did his voice become so quiet?

Officer Daniels nodded. "They are in a shared room, so that they could be together. You can see both of them, but they are both under heavy sedation."

Blaine nodded and felt as if his head would wobble off of his shoulders. More tears slid down his cheeks, and he could hear Justin sobbing. He turned and took Justin into his arms, trying to convey his heartbreak in the embrace. Justin held onto him, as if for dear life. Blaine didn't want to let go of him, but he knew that they had to see Poppy and Dava, that they couldn't avoid it forever, as much as he wanted to spare Justin any further heartbreak.

"Can you take us to her?" Blaine asked.

"Nurse Hoffman will take you," Officer Johnson replied.

They slowly filed out of the room, one at a time and Blaine couldn't help but be reminded of a funeral procession.

Chapter Eighty-Six

Blaine didn't know what to expect when he walked into the room, but it wasn't seeing Poppy this way. She was lying in a hospital bed looking like death warmed over. There were cuts and bruises on her face and she was covered in a white blanket. There were red splotches on the blanket, Blaine assumed from further bleeding.

Poppy was normally so incredibly full of life. One of the reasons they had been friends for as long as they had was that she never failed to amaze him. He had rarely known someone to live life the way she did, as if it was simply what one did in order to breathe.

In a bed beside her, Dava didn't look much better. There were cuts on her face and one eye was blackened and swollen shut. She was breathing the shallow breath of sleep.

He didn't know Dava that well, but she had clearly done all she could do to protect Poppy and he loved her for that.

Justin held his hand tightly as they walked towards Poppy's bed. Blaine heard Justin crying softly. Blaine was crying on the inside, knowing that no amount of tears would be able to express the sadness he felt at seeing his heart sister lying there like that. He reached out with his free hand and softly touched her cheek.

At the touch, Poppy's eyes began to flutter. When they opened, Blaine could see the pain there, the hollowness within her. She cleared her throat and said, "Hey ladies." There was a flicker of a smile and then it was gone.

"I didn't mean to wake you."

"I'm glad you did. I'm happy it's you and you too, Justin. I'm happy it's the both of you. Not another fucking doctor. I just can't take another fucking doctor right now."

Blaine motioned to Dava. "How is she?"

"What a fucking trooper. She tried to take Fred on. She tried to kick his ass, my warrior queen. My absolute fucking champion."

Poppy stretched out a hand to clasp one of Dava's, only for a moment. The gesture seemed to bring her strength. She looked back to Blaine and Justin. "So, how about that generic sports team, huh?"

"Honey, you don't need to make us laugh," Justin said.

"What about me, then? I want to laugh; I need to laugh. I don't know if I've ever needed it more."

"You need to grieve, Pops. You have to," Blaine said.

"I don't have to do anything. I just want to make sure that Dava is all right."

"Poppy…" Blaine crouched lower so that he was looking in her eyes, so dead and gone.

"I'm just so fucking sad. There aren't words for what I'm feeling right now. My baby was taken from me." She looked at Justin and held out a hand to him. "Our baby was taken. The doctors told me that it was too small to determine the gender, but I knew it was a girl. Our own little girl, Justin. Our very own little girl. I had already picked out a name. I was going to call her Josephine."

Tears slid down her cheeks and Blaine wondered if that darkness would ever leave her eyes.

"On the bright side," she said, "at least I can drink now. And God, could I use a glass of wine."

She broke into sobs then and Blaine and Justin moved in to hold her closely, as if to keep her from falling apart.

Chapter Eighty-Seven

Devon looked at Sasha with his mouth wide open in shock.

She grinned at him. "Just kidding. Well, no, not really, whore face. How many diseases do you have?"

Curtis, bless him, looked uncomfortable. "You don't have to answer that if you don't want to. Sasha, shush."

"Don't you shush me. This guy is sticking his dick into you and you're like my brother, so that means I get to know a few things, okay?" She tossed her hair. "So whore, how many?"

"None," Devon said.

"Yeah, right," Sasha shot back.

"Yup, get checked every six months, always used protection. Do you think I'm an idiot that just fucked guys with wild abandon taking my life into my hands?"

"I do actually. Nice to be proved wrong on that count. Thanks, whore face."

"I've been celibate for months until I met Curtis. I suppose that doesn't count for anything, does it?"

"Oh, it does. So, you're not a whore now, but you were one. And you know what they say: once a snake…"

"Sasha, that's not fair," Curtis said. "Stop being such a bitch."

"I'm looking out for you, honey. You've had lots of guys treat you like shit, who says that this one isn't any different?"

"Because he loves me." Curtis turned to look at Devon. "You do love me, right? Don't leave me hanging here."

Letting out a laugh, Devon took Curtis in his arms and kissed him softly on the lips. "I do love you. You've known for a while then."

"Yep."

"Were you planning on telling me anytime soon?"

"No, I was waiting for you to tell me first. It seemed the gentlemanly thing to do."

"You're assuming I'm a gentleman," Devon said with a grin.

"You are. You're gentle and you're a man. That makes you a gentleman."

"I love you," Devon said softly, kissing him on the lips again.

"And I love you, too," Curtis said.

"Um, hello? Hot girl standing here?" Sasha said.

"Oh, sorry sweetie, we were ignoring you until you stopped being a bitch."

Sasha punched Curtis on the arm. "I'm trying to be your friend. Friends look out for their friends. It's what we do. You pushed Derek away from me when I was seeing him."

"Yeah, 'cause he was using you for sex and getting you to pay his bills. The man was a fucking slime ball."

"Yeah, but he had the most gorgeous chest and his dick was enormous." She looked almost wistful.

"So, a hot chest and a big dick were worth thousands of dollars?" Curtis let out a little chuckle. "Honey, you're worth more than that. How about a brain to go with that hot cock?"

Sasha let out her own laugh and said, "Point taken." She turned to Devon and held out her hand to him. "Hi Devon, nice to meet you. I'm Sasha, and I'm not always a bitch."

"That's okay, you were looking out for him. I wish someone had done the same for me." Instead of taking her hand, he hugged her quickly. "Thanks."

Sasha stood gaping at him open-mouthed for a moment and then said, "See Curtis? He's thanking me for being a bitch! This man knows how to talk to a lady!"

Chapter Eighty-Eight

Blaine and Justin left the hospital room for a moment to gather their thoughts and to let Poppy rest a bit more. When they were in the hall, they hugged each other for a moment, taking comfort in each other.

"I'm sorry," Justin said.

"Why are you sorry? It was your baby. I'm the one who should be comforting you."

"Well, let's work on comforting each other, okay?" Justin said.

"Of course." Blaine kissed him softly. "Always."

"Always," Justin repeated.

"Come on, let's go find your mom. She's probably worried sick."

They went into the waiting room to find it filled with people. Cordellia was there with Joe. Romilda was there with Gaston. Mike was there with Nancy with William standing close by. Chuck was there with Sebastian and a young woman he did not know. There were also two grown men that looked so much like Dava that it was not hard to figure out who they were. Blaine wondered who had gotten hold of Dava's sons but assumed that the hospital had called them. Victoria was also with them and looking somewhat uncomfortable.

Nancy came towards them and wrapped his arms around both of them. Nancy smelled like sugar and something spicy, and the scent was so comforting to Blaine. "Honey, how are they? Is there anything we can do?"

Blaine sighed gratefully. "They're as good as they can be. At least they're alive. That's the important thing."

Dava's sons walked over and introduced themselves. Ryan

was a tall man with a large beard and kind blue eyes. Robb was a little shorter and had a goatee. It was weird looking into their faces and seeing Dava, but Blaine supposed that was what it was like for his mom.

"Is our mother all right?" Robb asked.

"She's under sedation right now, but I'm sure she'd love to know that you were here. Why don't you go in and see her? She might wake up soon," Justin said.

"Thank you for taking care of her," Robb said.

"We didn't do anything," Blaine said kindly.

"You treat her like family. She's talked about all of you quite a lot. Family takes care of one another. Thank you for that."

Robb and Ryan went to see their mother, and Blaine knew right then that he needed his own mother. Cordellia seemed to know this and came to him, enfolding him in her arms. She hugged him with all the might that she could fit into a hug then she turned to Justin.

"You too, son."

"What? I'm not your son, he is."

"That's where you're wrong. You two are getting married. That makes you my son, too."

She hugged Justin with just as strong of a hug as she had given him. When they broke apart, Justin had tears in his eyes. "Thanks, Mom."

Cordellia smiled and patted Justin's cheek with her left hand. Blaine saw it then as it caught the light. The diamond ring shone like all the stars in the sky captured in an instant. Blaine took her hand softly in both of his, letting the light shine off of the stone.

"When did this happen?" Blaine asked softly.

"The other day. We had so much going on, I didn't want

to bother you with something so trivial," Cordellia said

"This isn't trivial. This is amazing and a blessing. A celebration is just what we need now. It's exactly what we need."

Blaine walked over to Joe and hugged him, too. He looked momentarily taken aback but then hugged Blaine back. "Thank you for loving my mother."

"No thanks needed. It's as easy to do as breathing."

"It's too bad we didn't have any lemonade," Cordellia said. "We need a drink to celebrate and take the edge off of our nerves."

"I was hoping you would say that," Nancy said.

Reaching into his bag he pulled out a thermos and a stack of red Solo cups. "Special delivery. Vodka and pink lemonade. I had a feeling we would need it. It's going to be a long night."

Chapter Eighty-Nine

It was nearly morning and it was only the three of them left in the waiting room. Just Blaine, Justin and Victoria.

A doctor had come out and had tried to send everyone home, but they refused. Nancy had stood up and snapped his fingers at the doctor. "Sweetie, if you think we're going to let our sister sit in that hospital room all by her lonesome, you have another think coming. Shame on you. I'd tell your mother if I knew her number."

They had gone through the bottle of pink lemonade and vodka quickly, however shared amongst so many people it didn't do them much good. They only got a little buzz each. In retrospect, Blaine thought, this was probably a good thing.

They had spent the time reminiscing about how awesome Poppy was and how lovely she and Dava were together. Justin talked about when he had met her at the bar. How the two of them had started talking and gotten loaded.

"She says to me, 'Man you're fucking sexy. If I was into men, I'd totally do you.' So I told her that I would gladly put on a dress if that was her thing. We ended up going back to her place and…well, you know the rest. It was never supposed to happen, but I'm so glad it did. How can it be a mistake when I got to meet all of you and the love of my life to boot?"

Justin had taken Blaine's hand then, and Blaine swore he could feel their hearts beating in unison, together in body and in soul.

Blaine had gone in to see Poppy again and found Dava awake with her sons. Poppy gave him a watery smile. "Still kicking around?"

"Yeah."

"Is everyone else still here?" she asked.

Blaine smiled softly. "No honey, they went home just a little while ago to give you a chance to rest."

For a few hours, everyone had been in to see Poppy until the doctor put a stop to it, saying that Poppy needed rest and time to heal. Eventually, they began to leave. Blaine and Justin had promised to update everyone as soon as they heard anything. Nancy left with Michael, Cordellia left with William and Joe, Sebastian and Chuck had left with Sebastian's daughter Cassandra; now that one was a spitfire if he'd ever seen one. Romilda had left with Gaston, giving both boys a kiss on the cheek.

"You take care of my boy, okay?" Romilda had said to Justin.

"I will, and he'll take care of me, don't worry," Justin had replied.

Then, it was just the three of them. For a while, they sat and listened to the sounds of the hospital: the cacophony of voices, the sounds of nurses talking to each other, the quick tapping of doctors' footsteps along the linoleum, someone's voice over the loud speaker. Blaine was about to fall asleep when Victoria spoke.

"I see why you like them."

Justin turned to his mother. "What was that?"

"I see why you like them. They were a motley crew of people. People I would never have associated with. But they all came for her and for you, son. They all came for you, to support you in your hour of need. I don't know anyone who would do that for me, not even your father."

Justin was touched. "Thanks, Mother."

"Call me Mom, okay? Mother makes me sound old. Come on, let's go home. I can make you both a cup of chicken soup."

Blaine and Justin gave her a look. "What? It's what my mother always made for me when I'd had a shock to the system."

Blaine and Justin said goodbye to Dava and Poppy and told them that they would visit soon. As they were about to exit the hospital, Victoria said, "And Blaine, you must get me Nancy's number."

"Okay, but why?"

"Why, he's a genius with eye shadow! I've been trying to do the smoky eye look for ages and always end up looking like a whore. If I could get a few pointers from Nancy, I could find a new man in no time!"

Chapter Ninety

Cordellia sat at the kitchen table, idly clinking a finger against a martini glass.

William looked up from the couch. He was actually reading a book, something he hadn't done in years. Cordellia had told him to read it because it would change his life. He wasn't sure how reading The Stud by Jackie Collins would change his life exactly, but he had to admit it was pretty good fun.

"What's wrong, Nan?"

"Everything. Everything is wrong."

"That's not true. You have Joe, you have Blaine and all of us."

She sighed. "I know sweetheart. I'm just so upset over what happened to Poppy and Dava. The fact that someone could do something like that to someone else, a woman that he was supposed to have loved once…"

"I know better than most that people change. Sometimes love changes. It happens."

"I know dear." She sighed again. She clinked her fingernail against the martini glass again.

William put the book down. "I know you're upset, but it's barely after ten in the morning. Don't you think it's a little early?"

"Oh, it's never too early. Besides, I don't want a drink."

"Then why are you playing with the glass?"

"I just like the sound it makes. I wanted to hear something beautiful to get my mind off of everything."

"Are you seeing Joe later?"

"Yes, he's coming to take me out this afternoon. He had

something to do that couldn't wait, he said. He won't tell me what it is, though."

"Then you have that to look forward to. In the meantime, why don't we go somewhere and be fabulous? It's too nice a day to stay indoors."

"No thanks. You might be fabulous William, but I'm just old."

William stood and went to her. Taking her hands in his, he helped her stand. "You, young lady, are a fabulous pillar of strength. You kept Blaine and all of us going in our teens when we thought the world was out to get us. You were a voice of wisdom and you were always ready with a comforting hand or a swift drink. You're not old."

Cordellia patted William's cheek. "You're sweet. Thank you."

"So, what do you want to do? Where do you normally go to be fabulous?"

Laughing, Cordellia looked into William's eyes. "You're serious."

"I am. You've made me feel welcome and loved. It's time I do the same in return. What do you want to do when you need to feel beautiful? When you want to shine?"

"I usually go to the spa and have my hair done, maybe get a facial."

"Then let's do that."

"What, really?"

"Yes, really. We can both get our hair done, have facials. Do you have a brochure for the spa? We could have massages and mud wrap treatments, even get our nails done! My treat."

"But you're a man. You couldn't possibly want to do any of that."

"Honey, I'm gay. I've been having facials and getting my nails done since I was in my early teens. Hell, I think I was making myself pretty in the womb!"

Chapter Ninety-One

Justin was trying to remember to breathe.

Ultimately, all that mattered was that Poppy and Dava were still alive. That they were okay—well, he didn't know if they would be okay for a while. He had no idea what it felt like to have a life inside of you suddenly grow still. He wondered if it was like a small voice that had immediately stopped speaking.

Blaine was out. He had needed to cover a co-worker's shift at the call centre. Justin didn't know why he did that kind of work; but then again, Blaine didn't understand his being a lawyer. He supposed they found a way to help others in their own way.

Justin heard the clink of a spoon, then the click of high heels. Victoria walked into the room carrying a tray laden with tea cups, a pot of tea, and some cakes. "Where'd you get the cakes?" he asked.

"A lady never reveals her secrets," Victoria said with a wink. She set the tray on the coffee table and sat down beside him. "Drink up."

"Is this another home remedy?"

"No, but the hootch I made the tea with is. It's strong."

"Mom, you don't drink."

"I do now."

Justin stared at his mother with wide eyes and mock horror upon his face. "Well, look at you, you saucy minx!"

What Victoria did next surprised Justin so much, he genuinely became shocked. She laughed. It wasn't just the polite giggles he had heard from her all throughout his childhood. It was a loud guffaw that started in the belly and just rolled out of her like thunder.

When she saw the look on Justin's face, she laughed even harder until tears were streaming down her own face. She took a few deep breaths and tried to calm down, but Justin didn't change his expression, and it would set her off again.

Finally able to get a breath in, Victoria sighed happily and took a healthy swig of her tea. "Oh goodness, I needed that."

"Mother, what is up with you? What happened with Father? What's going on?"

She took another sip of her tea and motioned for him to do the same. "I'm not going to drink alone. Drink up."

When Justin took his tea and had a sip, she gave him a smile and said, "Well, I suppose it all has to do with you, son."

"With me? I didn't do anything."

"On the contrary, you did everything. Do you remember when you came to our house and brought Blaine with you?"

"Of course I do, it wasn't that long ago, Mother."

"Well, your Father hit the roof after that. He went on and on about how he never wanted a poofter for a son and he would be damned if he attended some fag wedding." She grimaced. "Sorry, dear."

"Don't worry about it. What did you say?"

"Well, it was like twenty odd years of what I wanted to say came pouring out. I told him that you were our only son, our flesh and blood, and if we turned our back on you that would make us the worst kind of a parents imaginable."

"What did he say?"

"That if he had known you would turn out the way you did when you were in my womb, he would have made me have an abortion."

The air was filled with silence so thick, it practically snapped with electricity. Justin took an even bigger gulp of his tea.

His mother patted his leg. "Drink up dear, there's more where that came from."

"I'm sorry, Mother."

"Don't you dare. You have nothing to be sorry about. I'm the one who should be sorry. I spent so long apart from you that I feel like I don't even know you anymore. I've lost so many years with you, Justin, and I'm to blame."

"But Father—"

"No buts. I didn't have to go along with it or agree with him, but I did. I felt that what you were was unnatural, that it wasn't right. Yet, when you showed up to introduce us to Blaine, I realized that I didn't want to let another moment pass without you in my life. I told your Father how I felt."

"I take it that he didn't agree."

"He did not." She took a sip of her own tea. "Needless to say, we did not see eye to eye on things. How I put up with that stubborn ass for so long is beyond me."

"You love him. Love can help you forget anything."

"Loved, Justin. I loved your father. Now I'm working on loving myself. And you, if you'll let me."

"Of course." He put down his tea and wrapped his arm around her. "Of course, I will. What will Father do now?"

"Well, I haven't the foggiest. I've told him to get out of the house in a week."

"What?"

"Oh, you didn't think all the money came from him, did you? Oh no, it's all mine. I'm afraid without me, your father is quite poor. I'm pretty sure he married me for my money. But that's okay, without him, I wouldn't have gotten you."

She put her own tea down and turned to look at him. "Now, I'm not saying that this will be easy. I mean, finding out you fathered a child with a lesbian was quite a shock, but you and Poppy are alive and that's what matters. I'm going to work at being a better person and a better mother to you, Justin. That's my promise to you. It won't be easy, I have a lot of stuff to unlearn and a lot of new stuff to learn instead. That is, if you'll have me."

Justin hugged her and realized how frail she was, how thin she had gotten. Had she always been so tiny? His mother had seemed so invincible when he was growing up, like she could do anything. Now, here she was asking if he would have her as a mother.

"You have nothing to worry about. I'll always be your son and you will always be my Mother. We're in this together."

His mother smiled, a big watery smile that filled her eyes with light. "Thank you, son. Thank you so much, you have no idea how happy you've made me."

She patted his cheek like she used to do when he was a child. "Now, we have to talk about getting Blaine's canvas into a gallery. The world needs to see the beauty he creates! He doesn't do nudes, does he?"

Chapter Ninety-Two

Romilda sat on Gaston's couch, holding him close. She didn't know what she would do if she lost him now. She had no desire to undergo what Poppy and Dava had been through and it just made her realize what was really important in life. One of those things was Blaine, another was Cordellia, and the third was Gaston.

"Penny for your thoughts?" he asked.

"My thoughts are worth more than a penny," she said with a smile.

"Okay then, one hundred pennies. What's up, gorgeous? You've been so quiet since we got back from the hospital."

"Just thinking."

"About what? Don't make me tickle it out of you. Talk to me, Romy. I'm here to listen. "

She took her time trying to find the words within her and was silent for a minute but finally she spoke. "Do you know why I was so hesitant to love you?"

"No. Will you tell me?"

"It's because I didn't love myself, not really. I had spent so long having to hide who I was. I hid it from Cordellia, from the rest of my family, from myself. I told myself that it would pass, it was a phase, it was something that could be cured. I went to therapists, hypnotists, anyone and everyone. Still there remained this feeling that I wasn't living my life as my true self. I was so lonely, I had no one to turn to, no one I could talk to."

"So, what did you do?" Gaston whispered these words so softly against her skin, Romilda felt herself shiver.

"I did the only thing I could think of. I told Cordellia the truth. She raged at me, at how I was throwing away nearly fifteen years of marriage. I moved out and told my family how I felt, what I was thinking of doing. They disowned me, vowed never again to darken my doorstep. My mother turned to drinking, my father to drugs. They couldn't deal with who I was. I destroyed so many lives just so that I could live one."

Romilda hadn't known she was crying until Gaston wiped away the tears with his thumb. "What happened then, sweetheart?"

"Well, life went on. I went ahead with my transformation. It took a few years until I was comfortable with myself, but I couldn't love myself. I went to therapy again and joined a support group. I finally felt that I was at home in my body, but I still didn't love myself. Every time I came close, I thought of everything I had cost everyone else. I just couldn't get there."

"Why were you punishing yourself for everyone else's faults?"

Romilda let out a small gasp. "What do you mean?"

"They were the ones that couldn't deal; they were the ones who couldn't see you for what you really were."

"A woman?"

"A soul brave enough to do what she had to do to live the life she deserved."

"I wasn't brave. I was desperate."

"Desperation can lead to bravery, or vice versa. You did what you had to do. Fuck the rest of them. It's not your fault that your parents turned to drugs and booze, or that your family is prejudiced. They should be celebrating the wonderful person you are, not acting afraid of you."

"I love you so much, Gaston."

"And I love you, Romy. But do you love yourself?"

She nodded. "Yes, it took me a long time, but I do. I do love myself."

"That's my girl," he said and kissed her softly until it felt as if they were melting into each other.

Chapter Ninety-Three

Cassandra was sitting on one of the bar stools at the breakfast table, colouring. Sebastian looked up from his newspaper when he heard the pencil crayons scratching on the paper. "Aren't you a little old for colouring books?"

"Mom, they're all the rage, supposed to be all meditative and shit. God knows I could use some meditation after last night. That was fucked."

"Hey, language," Sebastian said sternly.

"I've been swearing since I was in my teens," she said. "Not that you would know."

Sighing, Sebastian set the paper down. "I told you I was sorry. I'm going to make it up to you."

"You can start by buying me a pony."

"What are you going to do with a pony?"

"Duh, I can ride it to work. I would save a fucking ton on gas."

Sebastian gave her a stern look.

"Sorry. Freaking ton on gas."

"Much better." Sebastian took a sip of coffee.

"You're a lot more frightening when you get pissed off as a man," Cassandra said.

"Is that a compliment?"

"I dunno, I guess so." She coloured a bit more before speaking again. She looked up when she spoke. "I'm happy that I'm here with you and you didn't have to go through this alone. Chuck seems nice. I like him."

Chuck was making breakfast, eggs and bacon with toast all around. He called it comfort food. He couldn't hear them over the sound of frying bacon and eggs. Sebastian looked at his lover and felt a moment of warmth that sped right through him.

"Thanks. That means a lot." He took her hand in his. "I'm sorry for everything that happened tonight."

"Why are you sorry for it? You're not the fat dumbshit that hit those two ladies. You have nothing to apologize for, Mom."

Sebastian winced. "Could you maybe call me Dad?"

"Nah, I already have a dad. I don't need another one."

"What about Chuck?" Sebastian could have slapped himself as soon as the words came out. He wanted to reach into the air and take them back.

"What the fuck are you talking about? You're not going to marry him, are you?"

Sebastian shrugged. "The thought did cross my mind. Justin and Blaine are getting married. Poppy asked Dava to marry her."

"That's them and this is you. Can you really see yourself with Chuck for the rest of your life?"

Sebastian didn't really need to think about it. All he knew for certain in this world was that Chuck made him feel whole, like the piece of himself that was missing had been found. "Yes, I can."

Cassandra gave Chuck a long look. "Well, you better get on it. If I learned anything about last night, it was that life is short. Plus, he has a killer ass. You totally need to tap that."

Sebastian spit out his coffee just as Chuck was bringing breakfast to the table. He stood there holding two plates piled high with food. "Coffee too strong?" Chuck asked.

"It's perfect, sorry. Cassandra was just telling a funny joke."

"It wasn't a funny joke. I was complementing you on your fine ass."

Placing the plates on the table, he said, "Why thank you. My bubble butt was a hot commodity in the gay community. Still is, but I'm off the market."

"I should damn well hope so."

Chuck went back to the counter to grab his own plate. Cassandra made a whipping motion at Chucks butt. "Stop that," Sebastian said.

"Make me," Cassandra replied.

"You're a little troublemaker, you know that?"

"Father says the same thing."

"What happened to Dad?"

"He's Father and you're Dad. Does that work for you?"

Sebastian reached out and took Cassandra's hand again. "I'm touched, babe."

"God, don't make me puke this early. You'll always be my Mom, I'll just call you Dad for now."

"I bet you were hot as a woman," Chuck said coming back to the table.

"Oh, gross."

"Oh, she totally was!" Cassandra said. "Wait, I'll get my phone. I have pictures."

Cassandra ran out of the kitchen leaving Chuck and Sebastian on their own. "I don't know who she gets it from," Sebastian said.

"I'd say the apple doesn't fall far from the tree," Chuck said with a grin and took a sip of his coffee.

Chapter Ninety-Four

Mike had to admit it, his whole body felt lighter. The ring ceremony had helped him beyond measure.

Though the shock of what had happened to Poppy and Dava had thrown all of them, being able to let go of all the hurt that William had caused made him feel like a new man. Mike had been carrying around the lost love for William while loving Nancy at the same time. It was a lot to have inside one body.

It struck Mike then how quickly life could change, how fast it moved when sometimes it seemed to take forever. He thought of the love he had carried for Nancy for so long until it was allowed to come out and breathe. Of how he had, even then, loved two people at the same time. Now there was only the love for Nancy that filled him, only the passion created with Nancy that drove him. Nancy had given him back his life and had shown him how to let his heart truly love.

Nancy was sleeping beside him. Mike looked at him, at his face free of makeup. He was the epitome of beauty, and Mike was filled with nothing but love for him. He wished he were creative like Blaine or Nancy, able to put what he felt into a poem or a painting. Able to convey to Nancy what he meant to him. He would do anything in his power to protect Nancy.

Instead, all Mike could do was love him as much as he could with all of his heart. He carefully stroked Nancy's face with the back of his hand and then leaned down to kiss him softly on the forehead. Nancy's eyes fluttered then, and he moved in closer to Mike, the heat from Nancy's body warming him.

"Well, this sure is a wonderful way to wake up."

"I'd say so," Mike grinned. "Good morning."

"Did last night really happen or was it like some kind of dream?"

"It happened. It wasn't a dream."

"Gods," Nancy said. "To think that Dava and Poppy had to go through that. I'm so glad they have each other now. Poppy has been alone for so long. I'm just happy they can gather strength from each other."

"I feel the same way about you."

"You had William. it's not the same thing."

"I was alone in the relationship. That amounts to the same thing."

"Touché," Nancy kissed him softly. "I'm so in love with you."

"And I with you."

"I was alone for so long. I had Devon for a little bit, but he didn't really want me. He just wanted a quick roll in the hay."

"I don't think that's true. He loved you in his way. He just didn't love you in the way that you needed."

"So, you're standing up for him now? The man-whore?"

"No, I'm just pointing out that everyone loves differently and maybe he couldn't love the right way for you. Love is different for everyone, you know."

Nancy let out a sigh. "I just hope he's happy. That's all."

"I know you do."

Nancy was quiet for a moment. When he spoke, his voice was thoughtful and calm. "I love you, Michael."

"I know you do. And I love you, more than anything."

"I'd be honoured if you wore my ring on your finger."

"What do you mean?"

"Life is too short. We should celebrate what is good in our lives, what moves us and unites us. You are like a light in my

231

life and I want to let everyone know that."

"Are you proposing to me?"

"No, I'm not doing that. I don't go in for the whole marriage thing. It's too much fuss and bother. Plus, I'd look horrible in white don't you think? I'm far from a virgin anyways. Let's just have a symbol of our love. That's all I want."

Michael was moved, incredibly so. He had never felt so much love for one person, so much emotion. He kissed Nancy softly, but tried to convey all his emotions in the kiss. How lucky he felt, how honoured he was, how humbled.

When he broke the kiss, Nancy was smiling at him and the smile lit up his eyes like lights.

"When do you want to go shopping for rings?" Mike said.

"Rings, as in plural?"

"Of course, silly. If I'm going to wear your ring, you have to wear mine."

A look of glee filled Nancy's face. "Oh! Can I get one with sparkly diamonds? Oooh, or maybe one that lights up?"

Mike let out a laugh. "We'll see what we can find."

Chapter Ninety-Five

There was a knock on the hospital room door.

Looking up, Poppy saw a familiar frizz of hair and knew who it was. Dava's sons had come to take their mother to the cafeteria earlier. Dava had improved and the bruising was fading. She had needed several stiches, but she was holding up. Poppy, on the other hand, wasn't doing so well. To have a life growing in her one moment and then to have that light snuffed out—she was at rock bottom. She was the lowest she could possibly sink to in life. That was why she didn't feel an ounce of remorse for what she was about to set in motion.

"Come in," Poppy said.

The door opened and in walked Connie Collins, or River Moon Falls as she liked to be called. She stood at the doorway looking at Poppy, an intense look of concern on her face. "How are you feeling?"

"I've been better, thanks."

"God, I'm such an idiot. Of course, you're not all right, of course you're feeling like shit. That was stupid of me to ask."

"Are we going to have this entire conversation with you standing at the door or are you going to come in?"

"Oh, of course, of course," Connie said, and she came further into the room and sat at the chair that their visitors had been using. "How are you?"

"You already asked that."

"Oh, shit. Shit, I'm sorry, Poppy. I'm not good at this sort of thing."

"Then how about I help you focus on something you are good at?"

"What's that?"

"Being a cold hard bitch."

Connie held up a hand to her chest. "Ouch. That hurts, Poppy."

"Do you deny it?"

"No, it just stings hearing it, that's all. Having it said out loud that way."

"Well, you are a cold hard bitch. Why does hearing the truth hurt?"

"Because no one's ever said that to my face. You're the first person to tell me that."

"Oh, believe me, everyone else thinks the same thing. They're just too polite to say it out loud, whereas I just don't care."

"You expect me to help you after this?"

"Yes, because it's the bitch in you that I need help from. Trust me, I respect you and that part of you. She was always rather frightening when you let her out in a boardroom. Will you help me?"

"Well," Connie fanned herself. "When you put it that way, you're going to make me blush. What kind of help did you need?"

"Well, you remember William?"

"Yeah, prissy little fuck, always sticking his dick into any hole that would do? I never knew how he and Michael could get on with each other. I mean, that's not a relationship."

"No, it's not. Mike is with Nancy now, and they are very happy together."

"Good for him. I always wondered if that Nancy-boy would find anyone to love him."

"Okay, pull the bitch back from insulting my friends, would you?"

"Done. So, what about William?"

"Well, he was with this other guy, David Jones. Do you know him?"

"Isn't that the fucker that beat the shit out of Blaine all those times?"

"The very same."

"God, this community is so small and incestuous. I fucking hate that guy."

"Good, I need you to use that hate. He's been abusing people again. There was this guy Devon that he beat the shit out of that Nancy was sweet on for a little bit."

"The neighbourhood bike?" Connie said with a grin.

"Yes, well, we hope he's okay now. David is after William now. He's hiding out at Cordellia's house for the time being. Do you think you could do something?"

"What kind of something?"

"Teach him a lesson. Give him a piece of his own so-called medicine."

"Sure, I could do that. Do you think Cordellia and William are safe?"

"They are for now. I don't think David knows where William is, or where Cordellia lives."

"Oh, trust me. Abusers have ways of finding things out. It's only a matter of time."

Those words made Poppy wonder who had hurt Connie in the past. What kind of scars did Connie have that she had never shown Poppy? "Well, can you be on the lookout? Just in case?"

"I'll do what I can. You have my word. If he even lays a finger on William or Cordellia, I'll break it off."

Chapter Ninety-Six

Cordellia was thankful for her life.

She knew she had made many bad choices, but they had all led her here, to this moment with William. Every choice, no matter how poorly thought out, no matter how badly done, led her to this moment; and for that, she was thankful.

They were both having a manicure. William was getting clear polish with some buffing, and Cordellia had chosen to go with French-tipped nails in a nice rose pink. She had gotten her hair done, and William had frosted tips put in his. They had also been pampered with facials and massages, and she felt fabulous enough to just melt into the chair she sat in. The nail artists had both left to let their clients' nails dry.

"Why have I never done this before?" Cordellia said.

"What? A spa treatment?"

"Yes. I always come here to get my hair done, but that's it, though they always offer me their other services. I've never taken them up on it."

"You need to start treating yourself more often, you know. You have a man to impress now, and you'll need to look your best."

"Oh, Joe loves me as I am."

"I know he does, but that shouldn't stop you. Did you know that every first date I go on, I always get my hair cut and my nails done? I want to show up giving the guy the best impression of me. Seems only fair if they are the ones paying for dinner."

"You assume that the other man will be the one paying for dinner, then?"

"Of course, they always do."

"Well, I have other people to think about. I have Joe to think about, I have Blaine and the boys to consider. There's Dava and Poppy, too."

"Nope, not going to win this one, Cordellia. You have to start thinking of yourself and treating yourself with kindness. I know you have Joe and a son who loves you and a family, but kindness starts at home."

"You're awfully wise for a young one."

"Young one with an old soul. You have to love yourself, first."

"Says the man who is with an abuser." She wished she could have taken the words back the moment they were out of her mouth. "Oh goodness, William. I'm so sorry. I don't know why I said that."

"You said that because it was true. But that stops now. I'm worth more than being someone else's punching bag. I'm worth more than just whoring around with some random guy. Look at what that cost me. I lost Michael. I lost him, and he's not coming back. I have to stand up for myself and not let David push me around. And I have to love myself. That starts now."

"Hear, hear! But how do I start loving myself now, after so many years of loving everyone else?"

William motioned around them with his chin. "This is a start. You have to treat yourself like the lady you are. After our nails are done, I say we go back home and have pink lemonades with a little something extra, get you all dolled up in a fabulous dress and make yourself sparkle for your new man. You're going to knock Joe's socks off!"

Cordellia let out a laugh that was almost girlish. "That would be lovely. Where were you hiding this side of yourself? Your quite lovely when you're this way."

"Oh, he was always in there. I just had to let him out."

Chapter Ninety-Seven

"I still don't know what we're doing here," Devon said.

They had said goodbye to Sasha, and Curtis had told Devon he wanted to take him to his favourite spot in the whole city. Devon had expected Curtis to take him to a meadow or some museum, but instead, he took Devon to The Cabin.

The bar was empty this early in the day, but the cleaning staff was in and Devon could hear the honkey-tonk music that Stacey liked to play while she cleaned. The outside looked different in the daylight. It looked like a hooker without her make-up on, all worn and tired.

"Why would you bring me here?" Devon asked.

"Because, this is the place where I first saw you. I'm pretty sure I fell in love with you a little bit then."

Devon laughed. "What, love at first sight?"

"Well, more like lust at first sight. I wanted you so badly. It was almost as if you swam around the bar, so confident and sure of yourself, what you had to give men."

Devon felt himself blushing. "I'm not that man anymore. I'm no one."

"No, you're not no one. You're so much more than that. You've everything a guy could want. You're funny, sincere, and actually have a lot of depth to you that not many people see. You're a good friend and have a kind heart."

"But wouldn't you rather have that guy who was suave and debonair?"

"Oh honey, there's nothing suave or debonair about whoring yourself. But that image of you? Meh, those kinds of men are a dime a dozen. I like the real you much better."

"Wow, way to go and give a guy a compliment."

"I am giving you a compliment. You just need to listen. I fell in lust with you that night, but I'm in love with you now."

The world seemed to stand still a little bit, almost as if someone had hit the pause button. The very air around them was charged with electricity and Devon could feel it snap on his skin. "What did you say?"

"That I'm in love with you. I wanted to take you back to where it all began for me. I would see you almost every night and just wish for a chance, wish for the opportunity to even speak to you. I wasn't brave enough, though."

Taking hold of one of Curtis's hands, Devon said, "I wish you had. "

"No, it wasn't the right time. You weren't ready for me, then."

"Is now the time?"

Curtis smiled, that brilliant and bright smile, and said, "What do you think?"

"I think it is."

Devon kissed Curtis with every fibre of his body and being. He put everything into the kiss, hoping that Curtis would know what he was trying to say. He didn't have enough words to tell him, there couldn't possibly be enough words.

But then it hit him. It was so simple. All it took was three words. Devon broke the kiss and looked into Curtis's eyes, that lovely mix of hazel flecked with a bit of green. "I love you." There was a feeling in his chest that felt as if birds had been set free from their cage. "I love you so much, Curtis."

Curtis smiled at him. "See? Sometimes, wishes do come true."

Then, he kissed Devon again.

Chapter Ninety-Eight

"I have to admit," Dylan said, "I never thought that this is what being in love would feel like."

They had indeed gone for a fancy breakfast. Dylan had taken her to the new restaurant in town called The Burnt Cactus and all their food was locally grown. When Rebecca had read that on the menu she had wondered out loud how they grew the eggs.

"What do you mean? Have you ever been in love before?"

"Oh, sure," he said. "Only three times in my life. But each time, it was work. Loving the other person was like a full-time job, really. One woman was full of drama, always bemoaning some slight of perceived insult. Another didn't want to engage in life, she was just comfortable at home ignoring the world around her."

"Hey, throw in a bottle of wine and a chick flick and I'm there."

"The point is, she didn't engage with her life, or the life around her. It took everything to get her out of the house, to go shopping for herself. It was as if something inside of her had been shut off, and she hadn't read the owner's manual to find out how to turn the switch on again."

"Some people are just like that. Sometimes they were meant for a few months, but not your whole life."

"It was her sense of quiet that drew me in, her sense of stillness. Then in the end, I figured that if she had become any more still, trees would start sprouting from her head."

Rebecca let out a loud laugh that was joyous and wonderful, much more like music than laughter. When she had quieted, she asked, "What about the third one?"

"Well, that was the woman that broke my heart."

"Oh, long tortured romance?"

"No, my mother. She broke my heart when she passed on. I don't know if I've ever forgiven her for that." Dylan held up his hand. "I'm sorry, that was rather mundane."

"It was, but it's the truth. I always want you to be truthful, Dylan. Plus, I think it's sweet that your mom was one of your great loves."

"You think it's sweet?"

"Sure I do. It's one of the things I love about you. That even though you're angry with Devon, you're willing to work things out with him. It shows how kind you are. I can only imagine how much you love your mother."

"You mean loved, don't you?"

"No, love. Love never dies. It just takes on a different form when someone is gone from our lives, whether it be from reaching their end, or another reason."

"This is one of the things I love about you. You have a different way of looking at the world. I need to look at the world that way."

"Plus, I can make a shopping trip into an Olympic sport. That takes skill and talent."

Laughing, Dylan took her hands in his. "That it does. So, who have you loved in your life?"

"There have only been two. The first one left me so fucked up that I lusted after a gay guy for years."

"What happened?"

"Well, we met at university. I was studying to be a social worker. He was studying to be a public service worker. It seemed like fate, to meet someone that had the same desire to help people, we had a bit of whirlwind romance, moved in together. You know."

"I do." He nodded and smiled at her.

Rebecca felt so comfortable with him, so at home with her hands in his that she decided to tell him what had happened. She had never told this truth to anyone else. She wanted Dylan to be the first one.

"I ended up getting pregnant, as it often happens. I was overjoyed. I thought of the life that was starting in my stomach and felt only light. Until I told Jackson. He was furious, God he was angry. He told me we both had our education to think of, that our degrees would get us further in life. That we had to focus on that instead of having a baby that neither of us wanted."

Dylan looked grim. "What did you say?"

Rebecca let out a snort. "That everything happens for a reason, that the baby was a blessing, a joy. We loved each other, so what was the harm in having a baby? We should be celebrating."

She looked down into her coffee and imagined that she could see her baby's face in the liquid, there one moment and gone the next. "He told me that if I loved him, I'd get an abortion. And I did love him, so I got an abortion."

A tear slid out of her left eye and fell into her coffee. She took a sip anyways. "Afterwards, when I told him, he was so angry. He said he no longer wanted to be with someone who would throw away a human life like it was nothing."

More tears were flowing now. It was her darkest and deepest of secrets and now it was out in the light of day. She heard how awful it sounded, knew that she was a horrible person to have done that to a life that didn't have the chance to grow.

Instead of pulling his hand away, Dylan squeezed hers tighter. "I'm so sorry that that happened to you."

She looked up at him and, to her shock, didn't see disgust or derision. Instead, she saw only concern and love. "How can you not hate me? After I did that, I hated myself. I hated Jackson, then spent the next several years in love with your brother so I wouldn't get hurt again. I hated myself so much. Getting up every day was torture."

"She's still with you," Dylan said.

"What do you mean?"

"Aren't you the one who told me that love never dies? Did you love her?"

"Her? I never knew the gender of my baby."

"Doesn't matter. I can picture you having a daughter. A spunky little girl just like you. You must have thought of names."

"Yeah, I did. Only girl's names because I was so sure it was a she."

"So, what did you call her?"

"Samantha," Rebecca whispered.

"That's a beautiful name."

"It helped that I was way into Bewitched at the time."

Dylan held up his coffee cup. "To Samantha."

"To Samantha." Rebecca clinked hers against his and drank the last of her coffee.

"Come on, let's get out of here. I want to take you shopping."

"It's okay, I don't need a pity gift."

"Who said anything about a pity gift? I want to take you out to celebrate what we're growing together. Plus, didn't you say that Coach was having a sale?"

"Yes," she said softly. "There's also this pair of black pumps that I saw that I would look fabulous in."

"That's my girl," he said.

Rebecca gave him a little smile. The world had not ended, even with her secret between them.

All she saw was love in his eyes.

Chapter Ninety-Nine

Cordellia walked arm in arm with William.

She had never felt more beautiful than this moment, well unless you counted the moment that Joe had proposed to her. Thinking of him sent a flush to her cheeks and a soft beat to her heart that filled her with light. She smiled with her spirit whenever she thought of him.

"Well, someone looks like the cat that got the cream."

She slapped William's hand lightly. "Don't be a flirt, you bad boy."

"I can't help flirting when I'm walking arm and arm with a beautiful lady."

"Yes, but I don't have the parts your looking for, dear."

"Doesn't matter. I know beauty when I see it. And you, honey, are beautiful. Come on, do a twirl for me."

"I'm not wearing the right dress for a twirl."

"Is there such a thing? Come on, twirl!"

Letting out a laugh, Cordellia did a graceful twirl, both arms outstretched and her smile even wider on her face.

"Fierce! You look like Lynda Carter in Wonder Woman."

"Oh, you are a flirt. I'm old enough to be her mother." She gave his arm another playful slap. "Still, keep talking. An old woman can use all the compliments she can get."

They walked a little further, and Cordellia's house came into view. There was a man standing in the shadows of her doorway. Cordellia felt William's hand clutch hard on her arm.

"It's okay, William. I'm here," she said.

They slowed their steps a little, but the sun shone brighter that moment as the man walked out of the shadow. Joe stood there with a brilliant smile on his face and flowers in his hands.

"I thank you for taking care of my lady, young man. Hopefully he's treating you well, Cordy?"

"Oh, you know how it is," she said kissing him. "Jet setting to Paris for lovely coffee and chocolate baguettes."

"I have to keep an eye on you, William. How can I compete with Paris?" Joe shook his hand and gave him one of his wide smiles. "I thank you."

"It was my pleasure," William said, trying to calm his nerves. He had thought Joe had been David, waiting for him, tracking him down at last. William knew it was only a matter of time until David found him and he was preparing for that, but he wasn't ready, not yet. He shook his head slightly to clear the image of David from his mind's eye.

"Plus, we had fun. We went to pamper ourselves."

"And don't you look like a treat for the eyes," Joe said.

"Thanks, I clean up well," William said, jokingly.

"Well, I was complimenting Cordellia, but you look very handsome yourself."

"I'll leave you two alone. I have to read more of that Jackie Collins book. I stopped in the middle of a love scene."

"Oh, Jackie can wait," Joe said. "I was going to take this lovely lady out for dinner and you're welcome to join us."

"That's okay. You go and be in love. I'll be fine. Maybe I'll see if one of the guys is free. Don't worry about me."

"If you're sure, dear? You are welcome to come along."

"No one likes a third wheel, Cordellia. It's all good. You two kids go have fun."

He watched them walk off arm in arm, the sun glinting off of Nan's newly done hair. But it was her smile that really shone brightly, the kind of radiance that comes from a woman who knows complete and total happiness.

He wondered if such a smile could ever grace his own face. Had he ever been that happy once? He thought that maybe he had. William had to believe that it would happen again.

Letting himself into the house, he walked into the living room and stopped. Everything looked the same, seemed to be in place, but for some reason William's hackles rose. His gut was telling him to run, get out, flee.

He was just about to head to a bar and drown his sorrows when he heard a noise from the kitchen. Something smashed and there was the clatter of broken glass. Then only silence.

Fighting against the urge to run, William went further into the house. All seemed well, but it was too quiet now after the broken glass. If there was someone in the house, a robber or a burglar, he didn't want to frighten them off.

William's gut gave an almighty lurch, as if someone had punched him, when he turned the doorknob to his bedroom on the main floor. When the door was opened all the way, he saw David sitting on his bed, looking so very angry that his blue eyes were slits in his face. At his feet, there were shards of broken glass picture frame, lying only a few feet away. It had been a picture of him and Michael. William saw that Michael's face was now only a mess of jagged white lines as it had been scratched away.

"Hello, William. Miss me?" David said. "You've been a very naughty boy. It's time to teach you a lesson."

Chapter One Hundred

Connie was driving back from the hospital and turning into the downtown core when she saw it—that streak of blond hair.

It could belong to anyone, but there was a feeling of ice in her gut. She had met David a few times when he was with Blaine, and he'd always given her pointers on her hair. He said it was too frizzy, she should take better care of herself, and how could anyone love fucking someone who looked like they had stuck their finger in a socket?

He had gone on about argan oil, or some shit, which gave his hair the beautiful sheen. She should do something to make herself look pretty, actually put some effort into it. This coming from a guy who normally had to pay for sex. Connie had dreams of taking a pair of scissors to his hair. Poppy had always asked her why she looked so happy when she woke after one of those dreams. Connie had smiled and told Poppy the truth, and they had both laughed over it. She had never forgotten David's hair.

Of course, it could be someone else. She tried to follow him but kept losing him. It was difficult to track a person on foot when you were in a car. She finally found a parking spot and got out, hoping that she would be able to spot that flash of gold again.

That feeling in her gut still hadn't gone away. It was intensifying by the moment. She was starting to freak out. She knew William was staying at Cordellia's place, so she would just head there. She still had the key on her keychain from when she and Poppy were together. She ran back to her car and got in, put the key in the ignition and started it, hoping that she wouldn't be too late.

She had never been one for praying. She was a woman of action, of doing, of making it happen for yourself. Connie didn't let anyone do anything for her. If she didn't do it herself, it wasn't worth doing.

Connie supposed this was why everyone thought she was an angry lesbian. In truth, she was an impatient lesbian. People were too slow when they did things for her, or they fucked it all up. That made her furious when she could have done it herself and the right ways.

She had to protect William from David. She owed this to Poppy, she had to make things square between them and repay her somehow for what she had put Poppy through. She realized that Poppy had felt alone enough in the relationship to seek the arms of another—the arms of a man no less. It didn't matter if Justin was a nice guy, Connie shouldn't have driven her away or to find love with another, even on a temporary basis.

Connie should have loved her. She still did love Poppy. There is always the one person in your life that gets away. The one person that your mind romanticizes, even if the relationship wasn't perfect. Poppy would be that person for her, that one who got away, the one who would always be in her heart.

She didn't love Poppy properly when they were together, so she would do that now. She would do what Poppy had asked and make sure that William was safe. It was the least she could do, the only thing she could do.

Connie pulled out of her spot and made a sharp turn, the tires screeching and that icy feeling deepening even further inside her gut. She only hoped that she wouldn't be too late, that William was okay, that there was still time.

That was all she could hope for.

Chapter One Hundred and One

"What are you doing here?" William asked.

"Did you think I wouldn't find you? Do you really think I'm that stupid, and I wouldn't come to collect what was mine?" David spat at him. "You belong to me." David glared at him and rose from the bed. "It's time for your lesson."

"You won't be teaching me lessons any more. I belong to no one but myself."

"You're forgetting yourself. You are mine, do you understand me?"

David lunged at him, pulling an arm back. William felt the pain, saw the light it created in his vision, blackness and shadows filled with stars. He tasted blood. His teeth had cut into his lip.

Something snapped inside of William when he tasted his own blood. He thought of every moment with David and realized that there had been blood through all of David's lessons. It was always William's blood, never David's. Always his.

Unlike before, the stars didn't go away but the blackness did. The shadows receded but the stars that were still in his eyes helped William see David for what he really was, a small little man with a narrow mind and a cold heart. There was no love there, no affection. There was only control.

William had been so lost within himself that he had let David control him, shape him into this mess of a man who was afraid of his own shadow. Well, it stopped now, right this instant. He would take back his life, his sanity and his pride and it started now.

Drawing back his fist, William punched David as hard as he could. David's head snapped back and William saw that he had cut his lip and it was leaking blood. Seeing blood on David's skin instead of his own was an odd kind of reward, but William would take it.

David's eyes widened in shock. "No one ever hits me back when I'm teaching."

"Well, there's a first time for everything," William said.

"Why you little bitch!" David yelled. "No one fucking hits me, no one."

David landed a punch to his stomach. Oddly enough it didn't hurt. Instead, it sent fire through the icy feeling that had been there, filling his gut with heat and flame. William shot forward and landed another punch on David's face. He heard the crack of bone and watched in almost translucent glee as David's head snapped back up, his nose clearly broken. More blood was leaking down his face now, joining with the blood from his cut lip.

"You fucking whore!" David yelled. "You dare to fucking touch me! You fucking dare!"

He pushed William hard into the vanity, both of David's hands slamming into his chest. William heard the sound of more breaking glass and saw shards of silver fall around him, as if someone had broken a star that had come to Earth.

David's hands were around his throat and the air was being choked out of him. The stars inside his mind's eye had intensified to the point where the stars were all he could see. He was losing consciousness, his vision becoming filled with specks of light and fuzzy black and white shapes, as if he looked at a video screen when the tape had yet to play. William knew then that David was going to kill him.

I will not go down like this, William thought. I will take my life back. This will not be my last moment on Earth. He will not take me, and I will live.

With great effort, William brought up his knee and felt it connect with David's crotch. David let out a strangled yell and released him, and William felt the air return to his lungs. The shadows cleared from his vision. He knew what he had to do.

While David was down on the ground, William began kicking and punching David with all his might. He tried to communicate the pain that David had made him feel with each punch and lesson that David had given him. Soon, he had lost himself in the delivery of pain, and words were coming out of his mouth that were a release in their own right, words that made no sense and sounded guttural.

"Fucking show you, fucking show you. Think you can beat me, take away everything I have? Think you can treat me like shit, like nothing? You're fucking nothing, you're worse than nothing, you're a sack of fucking shit."

William saw a shard then, a slice of the comet that had fallen to the ground when the star had smashed into a million pieces. He grabbed it and took hold of David's hair, pulled his head back by it and held the shard to David's neck.

"Going to fucking show you what happens when you treat me like nothing," William hissed. "Going to fucking show you."

There was the sound of footsteps and someone shouted, "WILLIAM, NO!"

The voice was like a slap to the face. William looked up and saw River Moon Falls, AKA Connie Collins, standing there. She had an urgent look on her face. "No what?!" he screamed. "He took everything from me! He took everything! He deserves to die!"

"I agree with you. Trust me, I do. He's a Grade A piece of shit and deserves everything that is coming to him. But you don't deserve this."

Confusion showed on William's face. "What do you mean?"

"You don't deserve to have your life taken away by killing him, William. You're worth ten of him, ten million of him. Don't do it, William, please."

It was the word "please" that undid him. Every emotion he had been holding in, fear, anger, sadness, came roaring out of him at that moment. He let the shard of glass fall from his grasp, blood sliding out of his skin from where he had been gripping it. It clattered to the floor and sounded like an odd kind of music to William.

He felt arms wrap around him then, felt Connie's warm embrace and heard her whispering to him. "It's okay William, I've got you, I've got you. It's okay." He heard the click and beep of a cell phone and then Connie's voice again. "Yes, I'd like to report an emergency…"

William leaned into her embrace. William realized that for the first time in what felt like forever, he actually felt truly safe. It was a feeling that he hoped would never go away.

Chapter One Hundred and Two

"So, which one of you bitches is buying this time? And it better not be me," Blaine said.

He turned to look at his friends: Nancy was with Mike, and Chuck sat with Sebastian. Poppy snuggled in the corner with Dava. Cordellia was with Joe and Romilda with Gaston. Justin and Victoria sat next to each other, with a free spot beside Justin had saved for Blaine. William was there with Connie Collins, an unlikely pairing but they had been thick as thieves for a while now. Saving someone's life had that effect.

Blaine marvelled at his family, for that was what they all were. They had been through hell and back, each of them, and lived. They were his family of the heart and soul.

They had returned to The Cabin. It had been four months since the attack on William at Cordellia's place. Fall was filling the air with swirling leaves and the winds were colder than they had been before. To Blaine, they felt like the winds of change.

"All the drinks have been taken care of," Cordellia stated. "No need to worry about that. And I'm not one of your bitches, I'm your mother." She smiled at him. Blaine marvelled at the change that living her life with love had brought in her. She practically shone, she was so much in love with Joe. Blaine turned to look at Joe next, at the love he saw pouring from him for his mother. Blaine was so very glad that they had finally been able to let their love bloom.

"You didn't have to do that, Mom. I would have taken care of it, I always do."

"It's all good. You've taken care of all of us often enough. It's your turn now. I asked them for a special order. Oh, here they are now!" Cordellia cried.

Two bartenders came carrying trays with fifteen large goblets. Taking one, Blaine saw that it was filled with pink lemonade. "What's the secret ingredient tonight?"

"I went with two shots of vodka per glass. I figured we could use the extra bump."

"I had an extra bump last night," Chuck said. "My ass is still sore."

"It's not my fault that you have sensitive orifices," Sebastian said.

"Manners, boys, there are women present," Romilda chided.

"I don't see any women. I do see a bunch of ladies though," Connie said jokingly.

Blaine cleared his throat. He held up his glass and everyone else took one as well. "We're to celebrate. We have much to be thankful for. Times haven't been easy, but we've grown and changed. So today, I would like to salute that change and all it has brought us. It has brought sadness, yes, but also much to be happy about and thankful for. So, let's all raise our glasses to change and say thank you."

They all clinked their glasses and said, "To change!"

When they all drank, Nancy said, "Look at you, being all literary and shit. I'm the fucking writer here, that's my job!"

They all laughed, and the sound was the happiest thing that Blaine had ever heard.

He marvelled at the fact that they could share so much joy with each other after so much heartache. They had a long road ahead of them, but that was life. And they had a choice: to welcome each moment and what it brought, or to run from it.

In Blaine's experience though, life caught up with you whether you wanted it to or not. They were all living proof of that.

Nancy's phone rang, and he looked at the call display. He saw his publisher's name. He shushed everyone, saying, "Be quiet everyone!"

They all quieted down, and Nancy answered the call. "Yes, hello?"

"Clarence! It's Melissa Mollina! How are you?"

"I'm pretty fabulous."

"Well, prepare yourself, I have some news for you! Are you sitting down?"

"Yes, I'm sitting down. I'm just having a few drinks with some family and friends."

"Well, you're going to need more."

"Why? What's going on?"

"Are you ready for this? Your book is going to premiere at the number three spot on the New York Times Fiction list!"

It took a millisecond for the news to sink in. "The New York Times?" He took a deep breath and saw Michael smiling at him, glowing with pride. "Did you say the New York Times?"

"I did! Reviewers love What's Love Got to Do with It? and they're saying they've never read a novel so daring and real. This book is about to go big! We're already running a second printing!"

"Oh, my actual God!"

"Yes, it is a religious experience, isn't it? There's more. We're going to send you on a book tour! Pack your bags, Nancy! We're thinking a twenty-stop tour, all over the United States and Canada. There is some European interest, as well. I hope you're busy working on your next book. Do you have any ideas yet?"

Nancy looked around him, at everyone he loved and thought of what they had all been through. "Yeah, I have a few ideas that I'm thinking about."

"Well, get writing! I'll call you tomorrow with more specifics on the tour and the review they're going to do in the Times! Congratulations!"

"Thank you so much!"

He ended the call and, for a moment, words failed him. Then they burst out of him like a beam of light. "My book is premiering at number three on the New York Times! And I'm going on tour bitches! I'm going on a fucking book tour!"

"Better than a fucking tour," Chuck said. "Even I don't have the sexual stamina for that!"

Nancy kissed Michael and thought that in this moment, he had never been happier. He never wanted anything to change.

Everyone around them cheered. They all clinked their glasses again and everyone drank deeply. Cordelia smiled and said, "I think we're going to need more lemonade!"

End of Life and Lemonade
The Lemonade Series Book Two

Acknowledgements

There are so many people who helped me in the writing of this novel. I wanted to take a moment to thank them.

Nathan Caro Fréchette and all the wonderful people at Presses Renaissance Press: Without you, the Lemonade Series would not have a home, and Blaine, Nancy, Mike, Poppy, and Chuck's stories would have remained untold. You honour me and my words, and I can't thank you enough.

Cait Gordon: You are awesomeness personified and a true warrior. The fact that I can call you friend is a blessing and a gift. You really are a kindred soul.

Dava Gamble: You have been an inspiration since the day I met you. You constantly fill me with wonder and awe in all that you can do. You are a light in my life and it is truly brighter for knowing you.

Kimberlee Rettburg: You are my constant Writing Sister. The bond we share was built with words, and I am stronger for that connection. You fill my life with magic and a constant flow of Magic.

Karine, Meaghan, Alexandra, Rachael, and Stephanie: You are my Heart Family and it is an honour to know you and have you in my life. It's also great to have you in my cheering section. You're all awesome!

Wonder Mom, Wonder Dad, and my Wonder Mom-in-Law: Thank you for your love, support, and guidance. When I lose direction, it's good to know that I will have you to guide me back to myself.

Michael: Words can't express my feelings for you. You fill my life with a desire I've never known and have made me a better man. Life is more wonderful, more magical with you. You have my heart and love; I can only hope they are enough.

Abut the author

Jamieson has been writing since a young age when he realized he could be writing instead of paying attention in school. Since then, he has created many worlds in which to live his fantasies and live out his dreams.

He is a Number One Best Selling Author (he likes to tell people that a lot) and writes in many different genres. Jamieson is also an accomplished artist. He works in mixed media, charcoal and pastels. He is also something of an amateur photographer, a poet and graphic designer.

He currently lives in Ottawa Ontario Canada with his husband Michael and his cat Tula, who is fearless.

Visit him here: www.jamiesonwolf.com

Did you enjoy this book?

CHECK OUT THIS OTHER RENAISSANCE TITLE!

Some Assembly Required
by Caro Fréchette

Graphic Novel / LGBT

How well do you ever know someone?
Louis has been in love with his best friend Laurent for
years. Unfortunately, Laurent is in a happy
relationship with Lily, another one of Louis's best
friends. After they graduate high school and start
feeling the pressure of adult life, however, Laurent
begins exhibiting really odd behavior, and it seems
Louis is the only one who can help.

http://renaissancebookpress.com/

Renaissance.
Diverse Canadian Voices

Renaissance was founded in May 2013 by a group of friends who wanted to publish and market those stories which don't always fit neatly in a genre, or a niche, or a demographic. We weren't sure what we wanted to publish exactly, so like the happy panbibliophiles we are, we opened our submissions, with no other personal guideline than finding a Canadian book we would fall in love with enough that we would want to publish and sell.

Five years later, this is still very true; however, we've also noticed an interesting trend in what we tended to publish. It turns out that we are naturally drawn to the voices of those who are members of a marginalized group (people with disabilities, LGBTQIAPP2+ people, people of colour), and these are the voices we want to continue to uplift.

At Renaissance, we treat our authors like family. We are all authors and artists ourselves, and know that their books are their babies. With Renaissance, the authors are involved in every step of the process and their input is highly valued, though devoted committees take on the difficult tasks of copy editing, designing and marketing to achieve professional results. The authors are asked to do a minimal part of the marketing (for example, sharing our social media posts, inviting their circles to the launch, participating in blog tours) and will receive guidance and help every step of the way.

At Renaissance, we do things differently. We are passionate about books, and we care as much about our authors enjoying the publishing process as we do about our readers enjoying a great, professional quality and affordable product on the platform they prefer.

For more information, visit us at renaissancebookpress.com.